THE SPIRAL KEY

THE SPIRAL KEY

KELSEY DAY

VIKING

VIKING
An imprint of Penguin Random House LLC
1745 Broadway, New York, NY 10019
penguinrandomhouse.com

Created by Dovetail Fiction, a division of Working Partners Limited,
9 Kingsway, 4th Floor, London WC2B 6XF, England

Edited by Jenny Bak
Design By Lily K. Qian
Text set in Albertina MT Pro

Library of Congress Cataloging-in-Publication Data is available.

First published in the United States of America by Viking, 2026

Manufactured in the United States of America
BVG

ISBN 9798217038947
1st Printing

for my friends, past and present

CHAPTER 1

IT'S NOT THAT I WANT HER TO SUFFER. I don't even need her to apologize. I just need to stop seeing her, because every time she breezes past me in her thousand-dollar Prada boots, every time I hear her laughter fluttering down the hallway, every time I see her sitting in the courtyard surrounded by bug-eyed admirers, I want to burn the school down.

"I know that look." Devin joins me at our lunch spot. "She's not worth it, Bree."

It's true. If Madison were worth it, she would miss me. Or at least pretend to feel bad about the whole thing. Six years of friendship should warrant that. But Madison never looked back after dropping me the summer before freshman year. It didn't matter that my dad got arrested, that I needed her more than ever before. She disappeared, and I went from laughing with a whole army of friends to hiding in the art room alone.

"I can't help it," I say dryly. "I love a public spectacle."

"Well, I don't," says Devin. "This shit is so beneath you."

I pop open my Tupperware, glare down at the macaroni. The courtyard is a perfect triangle, lush with grass and crammed with marble tables. Madison sits at the table in the center, surrounded by her usual group. Her silver-dyed hair ripples past her pale shoulders as she talks.

"We can go inside, if you want," says Devin. "We don't *have* to sit here staring at her."

"And miss the big reveal?"

Devin shoots me an irritated look. "Be sarcastic all you want. But you're doing this to yourself."

I'm not the only one. The whole school has been watching Madison this week, because this is when the invitations go out. Every year since starting high school, she's thrown the most expensive, exciting birthday party in the city—and I have never once been invited.

"I wish people could see her for who she is," I say.

"And who's that?"

The word *traitor* comes to mind. "I don't know anymore."

A dark-haired freshman approaches Madison's table. Tension tightens through the courtyard, draws up shoulders. The freshman carries a plastic take-out bag with both hands. Collectively, the courtyard stares. It's like a nature documentary, where the zebra is oblivious to the lion.

"Should we stop her?" Devin covers his face with his hands. "This is so cringey."

"No way," I say. "At least now they're not looking at us."

This is the worst time of year, when people are most desperate to get on Madison's good side. To appease her, everyone but Devin acts like I have a rare but deadly disease—like they're terrified to approach but still can't help staring.

When Madison posted a sneak peek of invitations on her finsta story last Tuesday, it sent the school into a frenzy. One word whispered again and again like an incantation: *Ametrine.* Ametrine, the multimillion-dollar virtual world designed by Madison's parents. As in, *I've heard celebrities visit Ametrine.* Or, *I heard Microsoft tried to buy Ametrine.* Or, *I heard drinking laws don't apply in Ametrine.* It's the only game that the Pembrokes refuse to sell to the public. A place created for one use and one use only: Madison's perfect party.

An invitation means more than an amazing night. Receiving one sends ripples through the school's entire ecosystem. The social order bends around who has one, who doesn't, who might get one, who almost did but didn't. It's all a game of proximity—how to get closer to Madison . . . and further from me.

Madison and her friends fall silent as the freshman extends the take-out bag.

"I heard you like La Famiglia, in the North End." Her voice doesn't tremble. She stands straight as an iron rod. "My dad went into the city this morning and I had him pick this up for you."

Devin groans into his hands, and I grip his thigh under the table.

Madison tilts her head. Her friends—Everly, Chet, and

Kyle—freeze, waiting for her reaction. Nobody moves until she smiles.

God, that smile. Clouds parting, angels screaming. The gift-giver relaxes. The courtyard collectively breathes out.

"Thank you," Madison says. She turns to the rest of us, and I swear we make eye contact for a brief moment. "I suppose this is as good a time as any. The invitations this year will, as always, come in the form of . . ." She reaches into her skirt pocket. "A spiral key. These keys represent unlocking the door to your future. It's our senior year, guys. My last high school party. It's going to be more amazing than anything we've done before."

She holds up a key so the autumn sunlight flicks against the metal. The teeth of the key are twisted so they look like screws. Fine. *Spirals.*

I was thirteen the last time we celebrated her birthday together. We ate Walmart sheet cake on her bedroom floor and watched *The Great British Baking Show.* Sour vanilla, stolen beer, laughing loud enough to shake the walls. This was before her mom's tech company exploded—before she became a billionaire-in-waiting and upgraded her social life. Before Everly and Chet became the center of her world, the ones she brought on family vacations to the Maldives and spent weekends with at her parents' mansion.

A low ache presses against my rib cage.

Devin whispers, "Do you want to get out of here?"

I shake my head. If we leave now, it'll be obvious why.

"Bree, come on," he insists. "Watching her drama makes you miserable. Can we just—"

"Shh!" I hiss. He's right, but it doesn't matter. Every September I monitor the invite list as obsessively as the rest of the school. I keep tabs on the gossip, the rumors. It's like if I keep track of it all, I'm more in control somehow. I did the same after my dad's arrest. *He wasn't only drunk, he was high on cocaine when he hit Mr. Greene. He's collected at least twelve other DUIs, and that's why Madison won't associate with their family anymore.* Like, if I have all the data, I won't be betrayed again.

Some aspects of the invite list are predictable. Her immediate squad is a no-brainer, and she tends to invite obvious choices like the class president and top athletes. She explicitly excludes me and most underclassmen. Then there are about twelve wild cards that she gives out and revokes at her discretion. Freshman year, she gave someone an invitation in exchange for doing her psychology homework. Last year, Robert Gray got their invitation revoked for sitting next to me at the lunch table.

Standing before Madison, the freshman looks sick with hope.

Madison turns the key over in her hands. She offers an elusive smile, meeting the freshman's gaze for half a breath, then looks back at her friends. "Everly," she says, setting it in her palm. "You were the easiest choice. You've always been my number one."

Anger gnaws through my chest. I dig my thumbnail into a crack in the marble table.

Everly's dark skin glows under the courtyard's attention. She makes a kissy face, hamming it up, and Madison swats at her, laughing. Then she reaches back into her skirt pocket and hands a key to Chet.

"Chet, you are my rock," she says, ruffling his blond hair. He scrambles to fix it as she turns to Kyle, the final member of her inner circle. "And Kyle. We took a chance, inviting you to the party last year. But you have totally proved yourself. Now I don't know what we would do without you."

Kyle's place in the friend group never made sense to me. I mean, he's a *junior*, and not even a cute one. Mousy orange hair, pale cheeks crowded with acne, his dark green uniform perpetually wrinkled. But there's no denying his status. Like everyone else in the inner circle, a streak of his hair is dyed silver, to match Madison's.

She hands him a key and glides back to her seat next to Everly. "This looks amazing." Madison reaches into the take-out bag, as if she might magically produce another key. The freshman inches closer. Madison rustles around theatrically for a good thirty seconds, then finally looks up at the girl, empty-handed. "Oh," she says, laughing. "You forgot the forks. Can you grab us some from the cafeteria?"

The girl's face falls. Everly and Chet burst out laughing.

"Christ," I mutter.

"Stone-cold," says Devin. The attention of the courtyard diffuses as people break into murmurs and turn back to their own tables. He stands, gesturing for me to leave with him. "You sure you're okay?"

"I just have to get through this week," I say as I shove my lunch into my backpack.

We slip out of the courtyard and back into the main building, navigating to our next class. Devin holds open the tall glass door for me, touching my back as I pass through. Inside, white walls blare down the hallway—no decorations, no inspirational posters. Even the lockers are painted a smooth, pearly white. It's a look that says, *This isn't high school. This is a training ground for the Ivy League.* Lincoln Academy doesn't have time for *colors.*

The air-conditioning razes down my back, goose bumps spreading across my arms. Devin pulls me to the side of the hall and takes my hand. He rubs his thumb between my fingers. "Hey," he says.

That's all it takes. Immediately I want to cry. Heat rushes to my eyes and my throat closes. I look down, blinking fast.

He tips my chin up. "Hey," he says again. "Look at me."

It never feels like Devin looks *at* me—he looks *into* me. It's the scariest and the most wonderful thing about him. Meeting his gaze is like peering over the edge of a cliff. My stomach curls up, my heart squeezes, and I can barely think straight because he's so unfairly beautiful, both feminine and masculine all at once. It's the kind of beauty that sneaks up on you, unflattering on camera but impossible to look away from in person. Freckles splatter along his cheekbones and his dark hair falls down past his shoulders. He wears his uniform with the sleeves rolled up, his nails painted purple to match my hair.

I raise my eyes.

"Thank you," he murmurs. He tucks a strand of hair behind my ear. "You know it's okay to be upset, right? Whatever you're feeling right now, it's okay."

"I'm sick of caring about her," I say. "It's been three years. Why does this shit still hurt?"

He draws me into a hug, and I press my nose into the warmth of his shoulder. He smells like Tide and pine-scented deodorant. I breathe in, out. In, out. His lips brush against my neck, then find my mouth. I kiss him back, gently. Sometimes I love him so much it's painful.

A yell bursts out behind us. I jerk back, spinning toward the sound. "What the—"

A gangly kid with a black ski mask over his head streaks through the hallway, winding between students. Startled shouts flare up across the hall as the figure sprints past, then screeches to a stop next to Mark Sato's locker.

Mark plays it cool. He always plays it cool—I don't know if he's capable of being surprised. Most kids here don't have to worry about money, but he's on a different level, second only to Madison.

"Hey, dude," he says to the masked student.

The student silently drops a key and a notecard into Mark's hands.

"Uh, thanks," says Mark.

Someone across the hall calls out, "Fourth year in a row!"

Mark raises the key with a bewildered smile. He moved here in first grade from Japan. He's always worn that same endearing, slightly indifferent expression. Even at soccer games, when the bleachers roar, even when he misses a goal or loses a game, his posture stays the same. Relaxed, easy grin. Loose shoulders, open hands. Madison has been obsessed with him from the beginning.

The masked student veers off, thundering toward the exit sign. Right before he gets to the door, he wrenches to a stop and slings a key at another student—some girl on the swim team. Vanessa? Veronica? I don't even know her name. But she gets a key, and everyone whoops in delighted surprise, and she beams like a pageant queen.

Devin steers me through the crowded hallway, then down the stairs. He jabbers a mile a minute about how it's tacky, actually, it's all juvenile high school shit, I shouldn't think about it, this will be over in a week and the party doesn't matter and I'll be shipped off to a kick-ass art school at the end of the year anyway, all I've got to do is hang on until then. I'm trying to listen to him, I'm trying to believe him, but everyone we pass is talking about Madison and her keys and her party, and honestly? I want to disappear.

We stop at his locker, and he pauses mid-monologue to examine the white metal. He's been in a silent war with the school janitor, a war that consists of Devin putting DIY climate action stickers on the outside of his locker and the janitor peeling them off. Neither will cede their position.

Devin scrubs his thumb against the sticker residue and sighs. "That bastard."

"Which one was it this time?"

"The bunny one," he says. "The one where it's holding a knife, and its thought bubble says 'become ungovernable.'"

"Rest in peace, anarchist bunny."

He spins the lock and pops open the door, cursing when something clatters to the tile.

"I've got it," I say, reaching down for him.

"Wait," he says. "Is that—"

Both of us freeze, staring down at what fell out of his locker.

A spiral key.

"Oh, for fuck's sake," I say.

He picks up the thick, milk-colored notecard attached, and I read the familiar loopy handwriting over his shoulder.

To Devin,

Welcome to Lincoln Academy. It's time we finally hung out!

Madison

He transferred here last year, so it's insultingly late to welcome him—especially because the school has collectively ignored him since he started dating me. He unsticks the key from the paper and rolls it between his fingers. For a split second, I catch a flash of longing in his gaze. Who wouldn't want to be invited to the biggest party of the year?

Instantly the nightmare spools out in my mind like toilet paper hurled into a tree: Devin hesitantly attending the party, then returning best friends with Madison's crew. Devin sitting next to Everly at their lunch table. Devin making jokes with Kyle, getting rides to school from Mark, circling deeper and deeper into their friend group. They'd convince him I'm a loser, that dating me is a mistake, and he'd doubt them at first but eventually realize they're right. We'd break up and he would discuss it with the crew at lunch, Everly offering sage wisdom and Madison smiling like a shark.

I'd go to prom alone. I'd graduate alone. I'd be entirely, completely alone.

Devin shoves the key in his locker and scoffs. "Not interested," he says.

But I saw the temptation, if only for a moment. He's never been invited to a party like this before. Anyone could see the thought forming behind his expression: *They chose me. Why?*

I have a good guess.

CHAPTER 2

SOMETIMES I FEEL LIKE I TRICKED DEVIN INTO liking me. Like I pulled some elaborate heist on his heart, and for the last year I've been waiting for him to realize. I basically did that to Lincoln Academy—begged, borrowed, and stole my way into a scholarship. Devin would say I earned it, that I'm a good student and a better artist, but I don't know. I spent weeks on my financial aid essay, twisting and turning it into the perfect cry for help. If I really deserved it, maybe I wouldn't have had to try so hard.

The point is, I can't stop seeing Devin through Madison's eyes. He's the perfect candidate for her friend group: puppy dog eyes, scary smart, dorky yet charming. He doesn't give a shit if other people don't get him, and he doesn't ever enjoy things casually. Like, he doesn't just play Dungeons & Dragons—he splays his walls with posters, collects colorful dice, watches hours of Critical Role and D20. He doesn't just listen to punk bands—he commissions T-shirt designs, runs fan accounts, and memorizes their tour dates. Somehow everything he does is cool because he's so confident in it.

Madison must be able to see that. Back when I knew her,

she loved board games with a similar brand of intensity. She hosted game nights at least twice a week, kept meticulous track of winners, regurgitated "fun facts" from the lore of all her favorite brands. It must drive her crazy that Devin is the only person who doesn't care about getting an invitation. He's the perfect challenge.

The perfect way to hurt me.

It feels like there's a bomb about to go off in my chest. Heat cramps up my neck, and my left eye won't stop twitching. Devin walks me to my next class, squeezing my hand and talking with a little too much energy. We pass by huddles of students in the cafeteria, fragments of their conversations snagging in a freaky loop: *key—Ametrine—Madison—party—key—Ametrine—Madison—party—*

Look, I can lose things. I can lose people and survive. If the last three years have taught me anything, it's that. But when it comes to Devin, I— No. I can't even let myself think about it.

He keeps his voice bright. It's not until we're standing outside the classroom that he breaks. "Look, I don't want to go," he says.

"No one says no to Ametrine. It's basically a once-in-a-lifetime opportunity."

"That doesn't matter to me," he insists.

"You don't have to say that."

"Hey," says Chet's voice, and I jump, nearly dropping my books. "You're blocking the door."

Chet's tie is half undone, his green sweater sleeves pushed up to his elbows. His blond hair arcs back in a perfect wave, slick with hair product that is strong enough to smell from across a room. Only one curl springs loose at the front, the streak that's dyed silver to match Madison. As usual, he's arrived with a mechanical pencil and a smirk. He twirls the pencil between his thumb and forefinger.

"Sorry, man," says Devin.

We're not really blocking the door. Chet could slide past us easily. But still, we step backward into the hallway, moving out of his way.

Chet slopes past us, then pauses and glances back to Devin. "I heard you're invited this year," he says. "See you Friday."

"I don't know if I'm—" Devin begins, but Chet's already disappeared into the classroom.

Devin offers me an apologetic expression. The warning bell chimes overhead.

"You should head out," I say. His last class is one of Lincoln's ridiculous "enrichment" electives: water polo. The pool is on the opposite side of the school, and Devin will have to run to make it there on time.

"Are you okay?" he asks.

I force an indifferent smile. "Never better."

"You're full of shit," he says. "But I'm about to be late, so I'll let you get away with it." He swoops in and kisses my cheek.

Warmth branches out from where his mouth touches my skin. "I love you."

"I love you too, weirdo." I touch the side of his face and his eyes flutter shut for half a second. Then he straightens, his hand brushes his pocket again, and he leaves. When I turn back to the door, I catch Madison staring from across the classroom. She looks away as I sink into my seat.

AP Calculus should, objectively, be a nightmare. The state test is notoriously soul-destroying, and I share the class with Madison's whole crew. But the teacher, Dr. Leon, makes everything worth it. I sit in the front row, right next to her desk. I can smell her honey perfume, catch glimpses of her narrow handwriting in her agenda next to the computer. For the record, I am entirely committed to Devin. But Dr. Leon is possibly the most beautiful woman to ever walk the earth. She was my bisexual awakening freshman year. I could spend days staring at her blue-painted fingernails, the hexagon tattoo on the back of her neck.

I slip into my seat, unzip my pencil bag, and organize my pens by color in a row down my desk. Madison sits a couple rows behind me. I sense her movements, track the lilt of her voice, even as I try not to pay attention. It's hard to turn off—too many years of practice. We used to have entire conversations through facial expressions. We'd be at recess talking to a group of people and, without a word, rise at the same time to leave. She'd glance at me over the dinner table, and I'd compliment her grandma's lasagna without any further prompting.

"How many keys are left, anyway?" says Everly, sugar laced into her voice.

"Telling you would ruin the fun," Madison replies.

A blur of movement jumps in my periphery vision: Chet's throwing his mechanical pencil in the air, then catching it.

"I just want to know who we're responsible for entertaining," says Everly.

"*We're* not entertaining anyone," says Chet, throwing the pencil again. It spins in four tight flips, then he snatches it out of the air. "Maddie's parents will take care of that."

Maddie? She hates that nickname. Or at least she did. How could he not know that? But Madison only laughs, and Dr. Leon strides through the door before the gossip can continue.

It's an easy class—another lesson in derivatives. I take notes and channel my focus onto the back of Dr. Leon's purple blazer, lose myself in the curl of her Spanish accent. She hands out the test results from last week (94—not ideal, but passable), and I tuck the paper into my binder to use for a collage later. By the time the bell rings I've almost started to calm down. At least I've stopped sweating. I pack up my things and half listen to Madison's crew as they discuss their latest grades. Somehow Chet swung a 98, despite never taking notes or doing the homework. Madison and Everly both got 90s.

"You're making me feel stupid," Madison complains. "Don't try so hard next time."

"I can't help being a genius," says Chet. "Actually, genius doesn't cut it. I'm a god. A math god. I can't help being a math god."

"You ate a plastic fork last month on a dare," says Madison. "And I wasn't talking to you, I was talking to—damn it!" She knocks into something and her books crash to the ground, papers spilling. She scrambles to scoop up her things, then they all shuffle out of the classroom.

I swing my backpack over my shoulder and stop by Dr. Leon's desk on the way out to ask a few unnecessary questions about the lesson. She compliments my test grade and reminds me to show my work. "I can't help you if I don't see your thought process," she says.

Fair enough. I nod and thank her, then start to leave when I notice a card under Madison's desk. It must have fallen out when she dropped her things.

Don't, I think to myself, but I'm already kneeling by her chair, flipping the card over. It's glossy, with a photo of Madison's grandmother Edie on it. My thumb traces over the words on the page. *In Memoriam*. A pang of loss bends through my chest.

Grandma Edie babysat Madison and me every day after school. She bought us ice cream and rented movies, gossiped with us about boys and bad teachers. I saw her way more often than I saw Madison's parents. When Mark asked out Everly, not Madison, in the fifth grade, Grandma Edie was the one to comfort her. When I split my elbow open in a bike accident in Madison's driveway, Grandma Edie was the one to dress the wound. I still remember the sound of Madison's frightened sobs—and Grandma Edie, gently insisting it would be all right.

A few months after Madison ditched me, I ran into Grandma Edie at the grocery store. Her gray bob glistened with hair spray, and she leaned against her cart for balance. She asked me about my dad, then demanded to know why I stopped coming around the house, and I lost it. I busted out crying, right there in the refrigerator aisle. She hugged me, the warmth folding over everything.

Now the funeral card stings in my hand. I should leave it. This—Madison, her family—it isn't my problem anymore. But Grandma Edie stares up at me from the card. I can almost smell her hair spray, a crisp bright scent like watermelon candy.

I'm not thinking about present-day Madison when I make up my mind. I'm not thinking about her expensive shoes or her cool-kid posse or her bullshit party. I'm thinking about ten-year-old Madison, the Madison with cherry lip gloss and a shared Claire's BFF necklace. The one who needed someone, anyone, to take care of her.

I grip the card and stride into the hall.

A sea of kids in green uniforms floods down the stairs,

toward the parking lot. I wind between classmates, catching a glimpse of silver up ahead.

"Madison!" I shout, and her head turns.

Shock breaks across her face. I elbow past a cluster of juniors. She's standing by the bathroom with Chet, Everly, and Kyle. I feel a hundred eyes on the back of my head as I approach her, and it occurs to me that it probably looks like I'm trying to suck up, to get an invite to the party. But it's too late to back out now.

"Um," says Everly. "*Hi?*"

I ignore her and set my gaze on Madison. I hand the funeral card to her. "I—"

Suddenly I don't know what to say. My voice struggles against the roar of passing students. "I didn't know about Grandma Edie. I just wanted to—I'm just . . ." I trail off. I want to acknowledge how big of a loss this is, but I don't know how. "Sorry," I finally manage.

Her eyes flick down to Grandma Edie, then back up at me as she takes it. She turns to her friends. "I'll meet you outside."

Chet, Everly, and Kyle exchange stunned expressions.

"Are you sure?" says Everly. "I thought we were going to—"

"I said I'll meet you outside," Madison snaps.

Everly scoffs, disbelieving. When Madison doesn't back down, she raises her hands in mock surrender, and they all head out.

"Come on," says Madison, grabbing my wrist and pulling me toward the girls' bathroom.

Dazed, I follow. It's empty, the smell of disinfectant tinging the air. Stress pounds in my temples. It's only the two of us, for the first time since eighth grade.

"I wasn't trying to embarrass you or anything," I stammer. "I was—"

"Thank you," she says. She tucks a strand of hair behind her ear. "I know this is weird. But I—I know that you get it," she says. "Grandma Edie was special. She didn't seem like the type of person who could die."

"I know. How did it . . ."

"Breast cancer."

"God. I don't know what to say."

"Yeah." We both just stand there, and it takes me a moment to notice she's turned, slightly, to go. "Anyway, thanks," she says, tucking the card away. "I'll . . . see you around."

She strides off, leaving me in a cloud of her acidic perfume.

I don't know what to do, so I go to the sink and wash my hands. My reflection wavers in the mirror: frayed purple hair, acne drowned under concealer. I catch my own gaze—and when my stomach clenches, look away. I rub soap over the spot on my wrist where she touched me, scrub it hard, until it hurts, then turn off the water.

CHAPTER 3

THERE'S NOT ENOUGH ROOM AT OUR WORN-OUT COFFEE table, but Aunt Lex insists on everyone eating in the living room together. She sits at one end. My little brother, Petey, sits on her left side, and I sit on her right. Mom stands at the other end, awkwardly leaning down to scoop up bites of green beans, because Lex still hasn't bought enough chairs for everyone.

"Sit up straight," Lex says to me. She was a Marine in her twenties and still talks like one. She dropped out of college when she was nineteen to follow her girlfriend to Berlin, then joined the military after said girl dumped her at the airport. Talk about U-Hauling. "Your spine will grow wrong if you're always slouching."

Petey's head snaps up. His blond hair flops over his eyebrows. "Really? Mom, is that true?" Alarm colors his voice. He's the most high-strung twelve-year-old I've ever met. "Is my spine gonna grow wrong?"

I glare down at my mashed potatoes.

"I was talking to your sister," says Lex. She runs her hands over her buzzcut, leaning back in her chair. "But it's true. It's the same with your face wrinkles—if she keeps wearing that pissy face, her wrinkles are going to come in all angry."

"I'm not being pissy," I growl. "This is just my face."

"You look like you've got a mouth full of lemon," says Lex. "What's going on, kid?"

Mom glances over at me from across the table. Petey feels the back of his spine with both hands, pushing his chest out. I wish they'd all stop looking at me.

"I'm fine," I say. "Just tired."

Lex grunts in disbelief. I stab my fork into a pile of mushy green beans.

"How are things with Devin?" Mom asks, in her I'm Here for You voice.

"He's fine."

"You should bring him around more," says Lex.

I look pointedly at Mom, standing at the other side of the table. We don't even have enough chairs for the people who live here, and they want me to invite *more* people over?

Lex is the opposite of a hoarder. It takes a supernatural effort to convince her to buy anything, and she's constantly trying to sell the stuff she already has. Every day she sweeps through the cabinets, the bathroom shelves, the closets, to pillage random shit to sell for a few cents on eBay. Still, somehow the house feels cramped. The extra chair for Mom is never gonna happen.

We didn't always live like this. We moved in with Lex

the summer after eighth grade, leaving behind a big blue house in Countrywood Court. I had my own bedroom in that house, a rippling green lawn, neighbors who went to the same school as me. Then Dad got arrested (and consequently lost his job at Tufts University), and Lincoln Academy shot up their tuition prices. Mom was adamant that we stay at Lincoln. Like if we dropped out, it would be admitting our lives were broken now. But even with financial aid, she couldn't keep up with both tuition and Dad's legal fees. So she sold the house.

Dad, being in prison, was in no position to argue. Two months into his three-year sentence, we packed our things into boxes. I left a pathetic note on Madison's doorstep giving her Lex's address, but of course she never came by. I don't know why I bothered. If she wasn't answering texts, she wasn't going to answer a note.

Aunt Lex accepted us with a suspicious amount of enthusiasm, considering how tiny her place is. But Mom makes sure that we're worth the trouble. Petey and I shovel snow, unclog drains, clean out the gutters. Mom cooks dinner and folds laundry—and in between scrolling on Indeed and ZipRecruiter, she stalks her ex-friends on Facebook. She used to have people over all the time in Countrywood Court. Sipping wine, gossiping, laughing loud enough to hear from upstairs. But those friends ditched her, the same way my friends ditched me. I guess some things don't change after high school.

Aunt Lex waits for me to respond, lips tight. I've been quiet for too long. What were we even talking about? Having Devin over? Petey chews on his knuckle. Tension spreads over the table, the air prickling like it's full of static electricity.

They're waiting for me to blow up on them. I used to do that a lot; I guess I had some anger problems. The kind of anger that takes you over, makes you say things you don't mean. Pulsing, scratching, clawing rage. It shredded my world into mismatched colors, everything tightening and peeling like a collage. I'd throw things at Petey, hurl insults at anyone who talked to me. I could look at a person and immediately know what to say to hurt them the most.

Like the Lincoln Academy counselor. I was sent to her the first day of high school, during my lunch period. She thought I might "need some support" after everything that happened. Staring at the hairy mole on her chin, I genuinely wondered if she was pulling a prank on me. All summer long, the only thing I wanted was to stop thinking about my father. And now, my first day back, she was pulling me out of lunch break—the one real time I had to try to make new friends—to talk about him? The hair on my neck shivered. My vision flickered like a television screen.

She asked me if I'd tried meditation. You know, to clear my head, deal with the trauma. I regarded her for a long moment, taking in her concealer-smeared wrinkles and thinning hair. Then I crossed my arms, smiled, gestured toward her face, and asked if she'd considered Botox.

She kicked me out of the office, and I never had to go back.

But this is all to say: I'm not like that anymore. I don't go around insulting people, even though I know how to. I don't deserve the look on my mom's face, like she's bracing for an explosion.

Then, thank God, Mom's phone rings from the other room. She nearly falls over in her rush to answer.

I speed through the rest of my dinner, hoping to escape before the family can resume their interrogation. There's a half-finished collage waiting in my bedroom, and all I want is to disappear into an art project. I stand up with the cleared plate and hear Mom's voice from the kitchen.

"I—I don't know. I can ask her."

My stomach contracts. I recognize that tone. If it were a color, it would be the navy that follows a disappointing sunset. It's the tone Mom uses whenever she has to deliver bad news, or when she's apologizing. It's the tone she uses whenever my dad calls.

She emerges from the kitchen. "Bree?" she says. "Your dad wants to talk to you."

I used to worship him.

He built me a garden in the backyard, dug out a square of dirt under my window and planted tulips. We'd sit outside and watch the bees as they landed on the petals. That's why he gave me my stupid nickname, Breezy Bee. In the evenings, he read

Petey and me the entire Narnia series, using funny accents for the different characters.

"Hey, kid," he says now over the phone, and I barely recognize his voice. "Are you there?"

I lean one hand against the kitchen counter. The family has gone silent in the living room; it's obvious that they're listening in.

I haven't seen my dad since he was released from prison last summer. Mom and Petey visit him every month or so, Petey sometimes even spending the weekend at Dad's new apartment. Mom tries to act cool about it. She's the one who made him move out, but she never badmouths him and she never filed for a divorce. I think there's some part of her that believes they can still make it work someday. But me? No thanks. Phone calls are the most I can handle. Dad insists it's fine, that I can take all the time I need, but desperation leaks through his voice every time we talk, and that only makes me want to push him further away.

"Hi," I say.

"Breezy Bee," he says. "It's so good to hear your voice."

Every year on the first day of spring, he'd let Petey and me skip school. He took us into the city for a day of browsing the Isabella Stewart Gardner Museum, eating cookies from Mike's Pastry, and lying in the sun at the Public Garden. He taught and retaught us about the Boston Massacre, the American Revolution. He had this way of talking that made everything, even history lessons, seem exciting.

"How are you doing?" he says. "I haven't heard from you. Your mom says you're applying to art school?"

Maybe if he'd been a shitty dad, it would be easier to forgive him. But the truth is, he'd been wonderful. He was never a mean drunk. He never yelled or threw things. Usually, he didn't even start drinking until after Petey and I had gone to bed. Later, Mom told us he hid the beer bottles and dropped them off at the recycling center to hide how much he was drinking. So when the police called us on that unseasonably cold June night, it wasn't anger or fear that I felt. It was betrayal.

He almost killed someone. Not just anyone, either—Lincoln's philosophy teacher. The most beloved teacher at the most prestigious private high school in all of Massachusetts. *My* high school. Mr. Greene had been out jogging and Dad clipped him, mangling his leg so badly that it had to be amputated. Now Mr. Greene uses a prosthetic leg and a cane to walk, and he frequently cites the accident in his lectures as a philosophy lesson in and of itself. I've never spoken to him, never taken his class. He teaches on the second floor, room 219, and I've built my schedule to be as far away from him as possible. On the rare occasions we pass in the hallway, I dive into the nearest bathroom and hyperventilate in one of the stalls. It takes a full ten minutes for my heart rate to go down, for the nausea to subside. The whole time, I'm imagining how it happened. All I can see is blood. Shattered glass. The smell of burnt rubber.

"I was trying to get to Bree," Dad had sobbed from the police station's phone. He was on speaker. Petey, Mom, and I huddled in the kitchen.

"What are you talking about?" Mom hissed.

"She was on the side of the road, and she needed me, and I tried to get to her but I—" His voice slurred, still bloated with alcohol. "She texted me. She needed me."

I had no idea what the fuck he was talking about. He was beside himself, delusional. I never texted anyone about being stuck on the side of the road.

"Bree got home hours ago," Mom said.

"What?" His sobs intensified. "She—but she—"

"You're drunk, Robert." My mom's voice never sounded so heavy. She gestured for Petey and I to go upstairs.

"No, Maureen, I swear—"

"You're drunk," she said again, and as Petey and I climbed the stairs to our bedrooms, I felt something close in me. Like a door, locking up. He was blaming *me* for this? It was suddenly, overwhelmingly obvious that I never knew my father. That he wasn't a god or a genius or even someone who had things figured out. He was a drunk and he was a liar. I was a pawn to him, and he wanted to use me to get out of trouble.

Later that night, Mom came into my bedroom and asked to

see my phone. I handed it to her in silence and watched as she opened up my text thread with Dad. Of course, there was nothing there about being stranded on the side of the road. Nothing asking him to come pick me up. His own phone had been conveniently smashed in the accident, so whatever proof he claimed to have was gone.

Mom stared blankly at the screen. In that moment, I hated her for checking. I hated her for not being sure—for questioning me enough to pull up the text thread and verify my side of the story. The hatred gathered like a bundle of needles in my throat, flexing every time I swallowed. Evening shadows tightened around my bed, darkened the side of Mom's face. I thought of Dad, drunk in his jail cell, blaming me. The knot in my throat widened as Mom handed my phone back. I hated her, but I hated Dad more.

Now, in the kitchen of Aunt Lex's house, I force myself to make small talk.

"Yeah, I'm thinking about art school," I say.

"U Mass has a solid program," he says.

"Okay."

"Or maybe Emerson, if you can get a scholarship. They do a lot of artistic programs. Film mostly, I think. I don't know what their visual arts program is like."

"Okay."

"How's your mom? How's Lex?"

"They're fine."

"Devin still treating you right?"

"He's fine."

"School going okay? How is it, hanging with the one percent?"

"It's fine."

"Great," he says. "Great."

"I've got a lot of homework." I start back toward the living room. "I should—"

"Yeah," he says. "Yeah, of course. Good talking to you, kid. Let me know if you ever want to—"

His voice cuts off as I hand the phone back to Mom. Petey reaches his hand out, begging for a turn. I don't know why he's always so desperate to talk to him.

When Mom passes Petey the phone, I don't stick around to listen. I leave the table, acid slicing up my throat, and no one calls after me. Nobody asks me to stay.

CHAPTER 4

I LIKE TO WORK WITH MY HANDS. POETS and actors are great, but I don't understand what drives them. I want to *touch* what I create. I want to hold the materials between my fingers at every stage of the process, and feel something pass between us.

Collages are best. Stitchwork is a close second. I like the way that collages demand destruction—that in order to create something new, you have to tear something old apart. You get to choose what stays and what gets left behind. After everything that happened with my dad, my relationship with collage changed from hobby to survival. It gave my work a new edge, an urgency that catches people's attention. I make a new collage almost every day, so many that we've had to start storing them in the garage because Mom refuses to throw any of them out.

Collage makes you an expert of discernment. I can't help but look at everything with an eye for reconstruction. A bad test grade doesn't have to stay a bad test grade; it can become a statement about fearing failure. Or a critique of the state education system. Or a metaphor for mediocrity. Nothing is stable, or certain, and that's okay. I can *make* that okay, because the artist makes the context. The artist makes the message.

Petey has a soccer game after dinner, which means that I'll have the house to myself tonight. I can spread out my collage materials and lock in. These are the best nights, when I can push the rest of the world out and be by myself, not because I'm unwanted, but because I'm *choosing* to take this time for myself to work on an art project. Ironically, these nights alone are some of the only times I don't feel lonely.

I lie on my bed and scroll through my phone as I wait for my family to leave. A few minutes later, Petey barrels through the bedroom door, looking for his shorts and running shoes.

"Are you coming this time?" he demands as he yanks a jersey over his head.

"No thanks," I say, not looking up.

"You never come to my games anymore," he says. "Coach says I could be the MVP this year. I'm the fastest runner on the team."

"I have homework to do."

"Yeah, right. Mac's brother says high school isn't even hard."

I ignore him. He shoves his face in front of my screen, widening his big brown eyes.

"Please?" he says. His hair sticks out in every direction.

A little laugh escapes me. He's too good at making a puppy dog face. I set down the phone. "Next time," I promise.

"Petey!" Lex calls from the living room. "Time to go."

He grins and races out of the room. A few minutes later, the house is mine.

I reach under my bed and pull out my art case, a shoebox crammed full of old exam papers, magazine clippings, and fraying ribbons. I spread the materials over the stained brown carpet and take a slow, deep breath in.

Time works differently when I'm deep in an art project. It bends, loosens. I'll look up and realize three hours have passed by. The house breathes quietly around me. I tear out phrases and photos, slather scraps with glue, place them carefully.

Bright, silver light knifes through the front window. Headlights? My family shouldn't be getting back for another hour.

I stand up and cross the room, peer through the glass. It's not Aunt Lex's beat-up Honda. It's an Escalade, engine humming, the windows sleek and dark. What the hell is a car like that doing in our neighborhood?

Movement flickers across the driveway and I surge forward, throw open the door.

"Hey!" I shout. Warm autumn air washes over my face. "Who—"

A dark figure dashes across the driveway, leaps into the Escalade. I stagger onto the front porch, try to get a look at their face, but they're too fast. The metal door slams shut and the engine roars. Is this a joke or something? I turn to go back inside, cursing, and paper crunches under my feet.

I look down. It's an envelope, sealed with neon pink wax. When I pick it up I notice the seal has a strange shape. It curls in on itself, like a spiral. Disbelief prickles through me.

The streetlights bear down, peering over my shoulder. All the tiny beige houses seem to hold their breath as my disbelief heats into hope. A dangerous, traitorous hope. Because this envelope matches the one that fell out of Devin's locker.

No way, I think as I slit my fingernail under the wax. A thick card peeks between the lips of the envelope. *There's no way she'd—*

My thumb catches on the paper. All the breath leaves my body.

Wedged behind the card is a spiral key.

A strange, shrieking laugh bubbles out my throat. I take out the key and hold it up to the porch light. Light flicks off its curved edges. Everything feels floaty, unreal, like I'm in a dream. A good dream. An *impossible* dream.

I pull out the card and laugh harder. The time, date, and address for Madison's party bulge off the page in silver lettering. On the back of the card, there's a message in Madison's signature loopy scrawl.

Forgive and forget? it reads. *Or at least forgive?*

CHAPTER 5

SMART LED BULBS BATHE DEVIN'S BEDROOM IN A silky glow. Every inch of his walls is covered in punk band merch, *Doctor Who* posters, and collages that I made him. A corkboard hangs over his bed, crammed with movie stubs and old Comic Con tickets. He pops open his third bag of Cheetos while I pace in circles around his bedroom. He's a stress eater.

"Theory," he says. "We have somehow tricked the ruling class into thinking we're cool."

"Disputed," I shoot back. "I talked to Madison yesterday, and she—"

"You *talked* to her? On purpose?"

"She dropped something in class and I— It doesn't matter. I went to give it back to her, and Everly definitely didn't think I was cool. She acted like she was Madison's bodyguard or something. A bratty bodyguard."

"Bratty bodyguard," Devin repeats, shoving a handful of Cheetos in his mouth. He sits on his bed, watching me pace. Bon Iver croons off a record player on his desk. "That's a solid band name."

"The point is, they definitely do not think we're cool."

"Okay," Devin says, lying down. His dark hair splays out onto the blue pillow as he surveys the ceiling. "Alternate theory: they are subconsciously attracted to us because, little do they know, we actually *are* cool."

I stop pacing next to him. His long legs dangle over the edge of the bed. I reach over and wipe a streak of orange Cheeto dust off his cheek.

"Respectfully," I say, "I think we can dispute this."

"Don't hide from the truth," he says. "We are *so* cool."

"Is that why you have a Rubik's Cube–shaped lamp?"

"I have a Rubik's Cube lamp to pay my respects to Mr. Ernő Rubik, the coolest creator of the coolest toy in history."

I return to pacing. My focus jumps from Devin's cluttered desk (a cacophony of markers, open books, and snack wrappers) to the knickknacks on his bookshelf (two Funko Pop! figurines and a deck of playing cards), then back to the desk as I speed around in circles.

"The thing is, Madison was different once we were alone," I say. "When it was the two of us she seemed . . . nice, almost. I think she wants to put it all behind us. Move on. I mean, we barely have a year left before we head to college. We'll probably never see each other again."

"This is the most exercise I've ever seen you do," says Devin as I stride past him again. "You're going to form a tornado in here."

"I'm serious," I say. "She seemed different."

"People like Madison don't change."

"But she *did* change. When we were kids, I thought I knew everything about her, and then she transformed overnight."

"Exactly! How are you supposed to trust her now?"

Pain stabs through my chest thinking about it. I sent her so many messages. Voicemail after voicemail, and she never sent a word back. Yeah, we were kids, but we had treated each other like family. I was there when she got her period for the first time, at summer camp in Cape Cod. When Paul Rodgers called me a slut during PE, Madison kicked him in the balls and got sent to the principal's office. I talked her through every fight with her mom, every disappointment with her father. We would have done anything for each other.

When we stopped talking, it must have hurt her too.

"Did she ever *explicitly* say that hanging out with me meant not getting an invitation?" I ask.

Devin's eyebrows shoot up. "Bree. Stop."

"I'm genuinely asking."

"She took back Robert's invitation for sitting with you at lunch one time. One."

"Yeah, but she never said that was the reason why, right? Everyone assumed. Maybe she feels awful about everything. Maybe she wishes she could take it all back."

He shakes his head, eyes distant. "She's a bully, Bree. That's all there is to it."

The kids at Devin's last school bullied him relentlessly,

which is what gave him his zero-asshole tolerance. It's also the reason he first started hanging out with me. He heard the rumors and tracked me down to say he thought the party drama was ridiculous, that Madison and her friends were narcissists, and I shouldn't have to deal with them. He invited me to sit with him in the courtyard for lunch.

It took months for me to trust him. I held back in all our early conversations, sharing only the easiest parts of myself. I wanted to be chill, easygoing. Someone worthy of his attention. But of course, he saw through all of that, and he never wanted me to be anything other than myself.

Still, even now, there's this voice in my head. It's on a loop, all day long. *What if he's been lying? Looking for the right time to leave? Telling people my secrets and laughing?*

I don't need a psychologist to tell me that this has to do with Madison. So why am I so tempted to trust her now?

"I know Madison is a jerk," I say, partly to remind myself. "I'd love to never talk to her again. But—I don't know. We were only thirteen when it happened. What if when everything went down with my dad, she froze up? Didn't know what to say, and so she stopped answering my calls?"

"She's messing with your head," Devin says. "You need to get a grip. She's only doing this because she thinks you're naive enough to fall for it."

Wow. Seriously? I whip around, a thousand retorts barreling up, but when I see his expression all the words shrivel.

"Sorry," he whispers. "That came out harsher than I meant it to. I didn't mean—" He winces, like he's expecting me to yell. I've never yelled at him. I never *will* yell at him. But his mom is a different kind of drunk from my father. She screams. She shatters dishes. She disappears for days at a time and doesn't answer her phone. Devin's dad sends a jaw-dropping amount of money to the house every month, but he never visits. I've only met Devin's mom in passing, on the way to his room. But in these brief interactions, seeing her asleep on the couch or hearing her shout at the TV downstairs, I'm reminded of why Devin understands me.

I climb onto the bed and lie down next to him. He pushes his bag of Cheetos aside and wraps an arm around me. My cheek slots perfectly against the crook of his shoulder. A feeling of total safety descends over us, a force field that keeps the rest of the world at bay.

"Do you trust her?" Devin asks softly.

Longing, dark and achy, stretches through me. Of course I don't trust her. But I want to. I want my friend back. I want my *life* back.

"I really don't know," I say.

"It's up to you. If you go, I'll go."

If Madison and I reconnect, I might have a real shot at feeling like I did before. Secure. Respected. Maybe even popular. I can't stop thinking back on memories with her. Hours spent sunbathing by her parents' pool, crystal water glimmering, the smell of coconut sunscreen. Bunk bed sleepovers, exchanging secrets in the dark. The memories keep shaking loose and sending ripples through my headspace.

Maybe when I gave Madison that funeral card, these same memories woke up in her. Maybe she remembered how close we were, how much I relied on her, and she twisted with guilt the rest of the day. She knows the power that she has. She knows that an invitation would change everything for me. Maybe she really does want to fix things before we graduate.

When I get home later that night, I open my laptop and send Madison a direct message over HiveMind. It's this social media app that Madison's parents bought around the same time that their VR gaming empire blew up. It's basically like Instagram, but with an AI chatbox built in. People are crazy about it. You can use the chatbot to edit photos, find weird new memes, stalk people you don't talk to anymore. Madison and I used it years before it became popular. As I pull up her profile, I consider using the chatbot to generate some conversation openers, but it feels wrong somehow.

11:54 PM

the_breeze_knees

did you mean to send me a key?

I'm not sure she'll see it—she doesn't follow me anymore, so it'll show up as an unvetted "message request." I minimize the tab and pull up Photoshop to work on a digital collage. Barely five minutes later, my browser pings with a response.

madison.pembroke

Definitely

I wait, hoping she'll say more, but she doesn't.

I guess I'm wondering why

I've missed you

My chest swells. I read that last message over and over again, searching for that familiar pang of anger, but it's muffled by my curiosity. I scroll through our message history. The last messages were from three years ago, all desperate notes from me. I cringe re-reading them.

Can we talk? Things with Dad are bad.

Everly said you're hosting a party next week, can I come?

Are you okay?

Why aren't you answering? I miss you.

Did I do something wrong?

Please talk to me.

I go farther up the message chain, and it becomes a stream of gossip, memes, and funny videos. Evidence of the good old days. I scroll up and up and up, delving into a lost world. God, I had loved her so much. It was all consuming, the type of female friendship that only queer people with hindsight can really understand. Love leaked out of the messages, bled through every picture we shared. We were just kids. We'd wasted so much time with this falling out—maybe it was all a stupid misunderstanding. Maybe we could finally get some of it back.

Screw it, I text Devin. Let's go to the party.

CHAPTER 6

I DON'T KNOW IF SHE EXPECTS ME TO bring a present. What could she possibly want that she doesn't already have? But I can't show up with nothing. It feels vital, somehow, that I don't reintroduce myself to her empty-handed.

I go into my closet and dig up the Don't Touch Me box. The peeling red cardboard sticks to my fingers. It used to be an empty shoebox, but in the summer after eighth grade I filled it with everything related to Madison. Old notes we passed to each other in class. Scraps of a history presentation. So many photos, all of us smiling together. I'd scrawled in Sharpie on the side of the box DON'T TOUCH ME! in the hopes that it would keep me from reminiscing, then shoved it into the back of the closet where I vowed to never look at it again. I don't know why I didn't get rid of it. Throw it in the trash, dump it in a bonfire. Maybe there was a part of me, deep down, that knew friendships like this didn't really end. Maybe I already suspected that Madison and I were bound to return to each other.

Maybe.

I sit down across from the box. The box watches me, skeptical. I clear my throat, as if preparing to speak in a business meeting.

Then I take the lid off.

The photo on top catches the light, glossy and oversaturated. Something in my chest softens as I pick it up. Madison and I grin off the page, arms around each other at the eighth-grade dance. This was the night she planned to make her move on Mark Sato, and she looked the part. Her hair wound into an elaborate braid that streamed down her shoulder. She wore an icy-blue dress and cherry-pink lipstick. Next to her, I seemed smaller than usual in my green dress. But God, the way I looked at her. It was almost worshipful. My mouth hung wide open, mid-laugh, as I beamed in her direction. Eyes wide, almost surprised, like I could hardly believe I got to stand next to her.

I rub my cheek, blinking. Then I move to the next photo, and the next. I pause over one from seventh grade, where Madison holds a crumpled piece of paper and glares at the camera like a bull about to charge. I'd snapped the photo right after revealing that the "love letter" she found in her locker was fake. I had written it the day before, imitating Mark Sato's handwriting. The letter included a long, cheesy poem; a printout of Madison's yearbook photo with hearts drawn around it; and the declaration that he was in love with her. I don't know how Madison didn't immediately realize I was messing with her. But she was seriously pissed. I laugh under my breath and push the photo back into the box.

I stack the other photos into piles, organize them out by

year. Then I go through the birthday cards, the notes, the secret messages. I trace my fingers over her swirling handwriting.

Sleepover tonight? In the bunker? I won't invite Everly

Mark is STILL STARING. He's so freaking gorgeous. WHY HASN'T HE ASKED ME TO THE DANCE YET?

Grandma Edie asked if you want spaghetti or chicken tonight

The hair place said you're only supposed to wash it once a week. Ugh. I hate when you're right!!!

A smile pricks at my mouth. Madison didn't know how to care for her hair back then, and Grandma Edie's beauty advice was wildly outdated, so she often came to me for help. My qualifications consisted solely of watching fashion videos on YouTube. But I learned quick, and I loved trying out different looks on Madison.

I pick out the best photos and arrange them into a circle on the floor. Madison and I posed together at her house, the park, the pool, the lunch table . . . it's obvious, looking at these, that we did everything together.

Not all of the photos are flattering, of course. It's funny, seeing Madison as a hormonal tween. Her braces glinting, cheeks smeared with acne. I want to include a few of these awkward shots in the collage too—not front and center, but haunting the corners, peeking out from under other pictures, subtly reminding Madison that I remember. I make another, smaller circle within that first one, using the old notes we'd written each other. Then I take a step back and survey the materials, searching for that familiar flare, the creative thread in my belly that tugs me forward and says, *This way.* Usually my collages come easily. I'll get swept into an idea and emerge only when the vision is complete. But this feels different. More risky. Both personal and outward facing. I need this collage to remind Madison how much we mattered to each other.

I need it to make her regret losing me.

I rip the edges off the photos with medical precision. I apply glue in straight, narrow strokes. The hours melt around me as I work. The softness in my chest expands, spreading down my limbs and encasing my body in a strange, warm feeling. Petey wanders in after soccer practice and I don't even notice until he says, "What's that for?"

I jump, accidentally slicing Madison's head off a photo. "Jesus Christ, Petey. Would you knock for once?"

He sticks out his chest. "This is my room too."

As if I need reminding. I sigh and stand up to study the collage. Petey scratches at his armpits. He smells like dirty socks.

"Don't we hate her?" he asks, pointing to the collage.

I open my mouth, then close it. I'm not sure how to answer.

"She invited me to her birthday party," I say, after a beat. "I think she wants to be friends again."

Petey gapes at me. "You got a spiral key?"

Ugh. Even the sixth graders at Lincoln know about the spiral keys. The mythos of Madison Pembroke reaches every corner of the known universe.

"Yeah, I got one," I say.

Petey crosses his arms. Ever since Dad left, he's had this idea about needing to step up as the "man of the house" to take care of Mom and me. I've told him a million times he doesn't need to do that. Devin even took him aside once, dude to dude, and tried to explain that it's an outdated idea, patriarchal as hell, and besides, sixth graders don't need to take care of their families—their families should take care of them. But none of it took. Petey's protective.

"You aren't going, are you?" he says. "I heard there's no laws in Ametrine. Anything can happen in there."

"I don't know if I'll go," I lie. "Maybe, maybe not."

"Let me see the invitation," says Petey.

"Why?"

He puffs out his chest again. "To make sure it's not a fake."

He's ridiculous. Standing there in his too-big soccer jersey, his brown eyes narrowed and serious.

Whatever. I'll humor him. I open my desk drawer and pull out the invitation for him to examine. I guess I'm a little proud, despite everything.

He peers at it suspiciously. "Hmm."

"It's real," I say. "I recognize her handwriting."

He holds it to the light, like a cashier examining a hundred-dollar bill.

"Jesus, Petey. Chill out. Give it back."

"Fine," he says. "I'm gonna take a shower."

Ugly, anxious thoughts worm through my brain as he lumbers off, the invitation back in my hands. What if he's right? What if it *is* a fake, a setup to humiliate me? But no. My hand tightens on the envelope. This is her handwriting. She confirmed it herself.

Definitely.

I've missed you.

I turn back to the collage, biting the inside of my cheek. The anxious thoughts pick up in a new direction. What if Madison hates the collage? What if she thinks I'm pathetic, desperate, stuck in the past? Everyone else is going to be giving her cool shit. Expensive shit. And I'm bringing this?

I pick up the collage, gazing at it more closely. It's a maze of inside jokes and shared memories. It's vulnerable, earnest, a genuine risk: An invitation back into my life. My version of a spiral key.

I nod once, to myself. Yeah, it's nothing fancy. But it's ours.

I have to hope it's enough for her.

Devin and I take the commuter rail after dark. Rain gushes against the windows. Most of the seats around us are empty, since people don't tend to travel into Boston this time of night. Neither of our parents know we're going into the city. Mom and Lex think I'm staying over at a friend's house. They were so delighted to hear I had a friend that they didn't bother to ask for a name or address. As long as I'm back by noon tomorrow, they'll never know.

I pull on a pair of headphones as Devin snoozes against the window. Madison's present sits on my lap, wrapped in yellow paper.

South Station is eerily quiet. A few late-night commuters doze on the benches, and a man calls out for spare change by the entrance. But otherwise, it's only us. We walk fast through the station and to the bus stop outside. Twenty minutes later, we're huddled under an umbrella on a dark street in the North End, outside an unmarked warehouse. The roads around us sit empty, all the streetlights turned off. A pigeon bursts into flight overhead and I jump, grabbing Devin's arm.

I recheck the address. This is the place.

Devin shifts from foot to foot. "We can still bail out," he says.

Water splatters off the umbrella. I clutch the gift tight. "No," I say. "We're in this now."

Seeing his worry somehow makes me *less* nervous, like there's only one person allowed to freak out at a time and it's my turn to be bold. I step forward to the tall black door, reach up, and knock.

It immediately swings open. Bright, white light pours out

onto the street, coating Everly in an angelic glow. A violet dress slinks down her frame. Pearls dot her collarbone.

"You're late," she says.

I glance at my phone. It's exactly eleven, the time printed on the invitation.

"Sorry," I say. "The commuter rail was delayed."

Her vanilla perfume brings me back to middle school, before she replaced me as Madison's best friend. Madison hated Everly back then. She would talk shit about her for hours, especially once Everly started going out with Mark. We still invited her to sit with us at lunch, but behind her back Madison was relentless, criticizing everything she did and calling her names, saying she was fake and only cared about boys. Our code name for Everly was F.S.—an acronym for Fugly Slut.

Chet emerges from behind Everly. Tonight he slouches up in a black blazer, dress pants, and turtleneck, with a cross necklace dangling at his throat. It's bizarre seeing him wear anything other than his rumpled uniform.

He lifts his chin to Devin. "Hey, man."

"Hey," Devin says, the surprise obvious in his voice.

For a second, my legs tense with the urge to run. What were we thinking, coming here? There's no way we'll fit in. Chet and Everly are both dressed like they're going to prom, and we're . . . I don't even know. A minute ago, my sweater and black jeans felt artsy, chic, cool without trying to be cool. Now it feels idiotic. At least Devin wore dress pants.

"Come in," says Everly. She reaches over and snatches the umbrella from Devin, shaking the rain off. "Everyone's waiting for you."

Inside, the warehouse stretches out into a wide white room. No windows. A set of metal stairs glints in the far-left corner, leading up to a lofted balcony. The walls radiate the exact same shade of white as Lincoln Academy.

The room is empty except for a giant table stacked with presents and a crowd of students milling around it. I do a quick head count as Everly walks us to the table: twenty people, including me and Devin. I recognize Madison's crew, Mark Sato, the girl from the swim team, and a girl from my world history class. Almost everyone else is a question mark. I add my gift to the pile, trying not to imagine all the luxuries it'll be competing against.

Anxiety squirms through my stomach. Madison isn't here yet. People keep peering around, like she might jump out at any moment. Chet tosses his spiral key in the air and catches it, the way he does with his pencil in math class. Mark Sato breezes over to him and falls into conversation. Everly joins, her dress trailing on the polished floor behind her, leaving Devin and me by the gift table. The other partygoers watch them, scanning for danger, like Madison's friends are flight attendants on a bumpy plane.

A few sophomores stare at me and whisper to each other. Everyone's dressed to the nines. I must look broke, pathetic. My face burns. Everly's high, false laugh bounces through the room.

Devin reaches out and snags Kyle's elbow as he walks by. They were lab partners, back when Kyle blew everyone's mind by qualifying for AP classes as a sophomore. This was before he got adopted by Madison's crew.

"Hey," Devin says to him. "How's it going?"

Kyle jerks his arm away, startled. His skin looks worse than usual, milky white with acne screaming across his forehead. It's hard to believe this is the same kid who starred in the school musical last year. His voice had soared over the stage, brought tears to our eyes, compelled even the most jaded audience members to rise to their feet. The spotlight cradled him like a proud mother. But offstage, he can barely make eye contact.

"Things are good," he says. "Excited for tonight. It really is a mind-blowing experience."

"When's the musical this year?" I ask him.

"Oh, it's—I don't know."

"What do you mean?" says Devin.

"I'm not—I mean, I'm—not in it this year."

"You didn't make it?" I gasp.

"No, I, um. I didn't audition. So. Yeah. I—anyway, I should probably be—"

"What do you mean you didn't audition?" says Devin, frowning. "How could you not audition? You were freaking amazing."

"I—I guess I didn't feel like—"

The lights go out. Darkness plummets over us and startled shrieks pierce the air. I seize Devin's hand.

"Here we go," Kyle murmurs.

Violin music wails overhead. The sound streaks in a circle around us, high, wild notes that make the hairs on my arms flex up. The lights blaze on again—barely long enough to see Devin's awestruck face—and plunge back off.

Then Madison's voice drips out, magnified through the ceiling speakers. "So glad you could make it to the party."

Silver lights explode through the room, rising in beams like we're at a concert. The music accelerates, filled out with driving bass and thundering drums. A gold spotlight careens to the metal stairs on the far side of the room, landing on the one and only Madison Pembroke. She shimmers. Green jumpsuit, three-inch heels, her hair wrapped in an elaborate updo. Bloodred lipstick. Collarbones you could cut yourself on. And God, that cocky smile.

She looks nothing like the kid I knew in middle school.

"Tonight, you will be entering a new world." A mobile microphone hooks behind her ear, magnifying her twinkling laugh as she descends the steps. "A world called Ametrine."

A shiver ignites down the small of my back. She smiles as if she can tell.

"To our newcomers: welcome," she croons. "And to our seasoned Ametrians: you'll have to forgive me as I explain our world again." She lingers midway down the stairs and leans against the handrail. "Ametrine is a virtual reality. A place designed for one purpose and one purpose only: the perfect party."

Cheers roll over the crowd.

"Since this part of the program isn't available for the public, you'll need to sign a quick NDA," she continues. Kyle, Chet, and Everly split into three different directions, each holding an iPad and stylus. People scramble to sign it. "My parents are so happy to have new players testing out this world. No night in Ametrine is the same. This party will last twelve hours, and every second of this experience will be memorable. I promise."

For a moment, her eyes lock on mine. I search for a glimmer of familiarity, a spark of recognition—anything to show that she's the same kid I grew up with. Her smile widens. Is she doing the same thing to me?

Everly nudges the iPad toward me. I take the stylus and scroll to the bottom to sign.

Madison reaches the final step and walks toward us, her heels clicking. "Now for the fun part."

She presses her watch with a big, exaggerated click. The back doors of the warehouse groan and slide open, revealing another section of the building. I follow the crowd into the room, Madison leading the way.

Tall glass cylinders tower around us. The one nearest to me is labeled VANESSA CALLAHAN, the one next to it MARK SATO—

and a few down from that, BREE BENSON. I touch the glass. These must be the VR consoles. A strange ache tightens my throat.

One of the freshmen tries the door of their console, but it doesn't open.

"Of course, to unlock the console, you'll need your spiral key." To demonstrate, she raises one key in the air and inserts it into the lock on her console. The door hisses, then springs open. "But wait. Before you open your door, there's one more step."

Chet and Everly share knowing smirks.

"Strip," Madison says.

Disbelief scatters through the group.

"Take off your clothes," she says, wearing a cold smile. "Now. Or go home."

She can't be serious. But around me, people are pulling off their jackets and their shirts without hesitation. Chet tosses his turtleneck at Kyle, biceps rippling. Kyle tugs off his shorts with shaky hands, revealing navy blue boxers.

Devin looks over at me, sending a silent question. *Do we have to?*

No one has ever left the party before getting into Ametrine. The shortest time someone has ever spent *in* Ametrine was five minutes, a kid named Jake Brown. Everyone hated him for wasting the invitation. Vicious comments have been swirling for the past year.

If I really want things to change at school, I have to get in and stay the whole time.

I pull off my sweater. At least I wore one of my nicer bras tonight, a lacy green one. I unbutton my jeans and slide them off my ankles, goose bumps pricking over my thighs. Devin hesitantly undresses beside me.

It's hard not to stare at all the others, especially Madison. She unzips her jumpsuit with a dramatic flair, the emerald folds rippling down to her feet. Then she opens her console, reaches inside, and pulls out a white bodysuit.

"Everyone here has a custom-designed haptic suit," she says. "They're skintight, head to toe, and allow you to touch, smell, hear, and feel everything in the simulation. There are goggles for the visuals. Even smells will be piped in through your console and into your mouth guard, clinically designed to invoke taste."

"This doesn't creep you out?" Devin hisses to me, and I shush him.

"You may now access your console," Madison says. "See you on the other side."

The key tingles between my knuckles. I'm so excited I can hardly think straight. This is it. A way in, after three years of torture. A chance at salvaging what's left of high school.

I unlock the console and step in. The doors shuttle closed behind me. My haptic suit sits folded on the ground. It's thick and lined with wires under the fabric. I step into it and pull it up over my shoulders. The suction cups inside squelch onto my skin, sending out little electric sparks. The back of the suit snaps into the console automatically, the straps tightening.

I meet Devin's eyes in the console next to mine. The look on his face asks, *Are you ready?*

I am. I have to be.

Sweat prickles under my suit. I reach forward to test the door, but then Madison's voice cuts through the console speakers. "It's time to enter Ametrine. You'll find the goggles charging in your console. Unplug them and press the power button on the side. When the button flashes green, put them over your eyes."

Nervous excitement coils in my gut as I reach for the goggles. They're oddly light, about the weight of an envelope. I click the button on the side and lick my lips as the light turns red, then orange.

Finally, the button turns green. I fasten the strap around my head, raise the goggles to my eyes, and—

Disappear.

My body evaporates. The floor evaporates. I hang, suspended, in sheet-white blankness.

No sound. No color.

No me.

I raise a hand in front of my eyes. I tell it to move, to make itself visible. But there's nothing there.

Devin, I try to say, but my mouth is gone.

CHAPTER 7

MY FEET SLAM INTO STONE.

Pain—we can feel *pain* here?—shoots up my ankles, splinters through my shins, and I fall forward onto my knees. Color explodes across my vision. Dizzy, impossible brightness. And—my hands. I can see my hands. They're braced against the ground. They look like real hands. Like *my* hands. The same cheap silver rings glint off my thumb. Every freckle lines up.

Cool fingers close around my arm and lift me to my feet. I follow the fingers to the wrist, to the arm, to the face—Madison's face. Madison's—avatar? It looks exactly like her, except *more* so. Like Madison, with the contrast turned up. Her silver hair floats as if underwater. Edgy gold piercings line her ears.

"Glad you could make it," she says. Her teeth glitter. A new spiral key tattoo snakes out from under the strap of her green jumpsuit.

I stagger back and turn in a circle, taking it in. Skyscrapers sway around us, reaching so high that I can't see their tops. The sky beams relentlessly blue.

Years ago, Madison and I lay side by side in my backyard.

She asked me where I would go, if I could go anywhere. I thought for a long time, feeling the grass prickle against my thighs. "New York City," I told her. But not the real New York. I'd been there before, for a weekend trip with my mom, and it was too loud, too angry of a place. No, I wanted the lore of New York, the *idea* of it. A New York that was *ours*.

It wasn't the truth. The truth was that I didn't want to be anywhere except where I was: side by side in the itchy grass with my best friend, twelve years old and daydreaming in tandem.

"What would make New York City ours?" She raised one fist to shield her eyes from the sun.

My dad's garden wavered in the warm breeze, the plants reaching toward us. I didn't know what to say, so I pulled from what was around us.

"Plants," I said. "Plants, everywhere."

Here, in Ametrine, flowers frame every window. Vines run down the walls and into the street, racing over the cobblestone and winding around streetlights, tangled and in bloom. My nose tingles with the smell of oranges and pine and fried street food—all the scents somehow distinct from one another, never overlapping or overwhelming.

"New York is too gray," she had agreed. "Ours should be colorful. And no cars honking at you all the time."

"How would people get around, then?"

She'd tapped her fingers together like an evil villain, plotting. "Motorcycles only."

I step backward, staring up at the buildings, and nearly collide with a guy on an orange sports bike. He swerves around me, rock music blasting off his speakers, and howls with laughter. He's as specific and real as anyone I've encountered in real life.

"Careful," says a familiar voice, and I whip around.

Devin.

I didn't think he could get any more beautiful. Coal-black lashes, sharp cheekbones, and God, that mouth. I would wage wars for that mouth. Pink and soft and curled up with new confidence.

"Hey." He brushes his thumb against my cheek. The touch warms me to my center. "What?" he says, smirking.

I look around us, unable to find the words. Does Madison even know what she's done? It seems impossible that this is a coincidence. After that day in the grass, I became obsessed with our imaginary city. I filled journal after journal with maps, sketches, characters, and presented them to Madison for approval. She gave critiques, asked questions, and I answered with more drawings. Before I discovered collage, this city was my haven, my alternate reality. A place I had to bleach from my mind after Madison and I stopped talking, because it was too painful to remember. And now she's made it real.

I turn back to Madison and find her watching me. I tilt my head, try to send her a telepathic message the way we used to. Her eyes go soft. She nods, once.

Tears well up before I can stop them. She created Ametrine for me. For us. After all this time, she remembers—and she's invited me to remember too.

"Welcome, welcome," she calls out, snapping back to business mode.

We form a semicircle on the street. Motorcyclists part around us, streaming by and infusing the air with joyful whoops. As the group exchanges baffled expressions, Madison calls over the ruckus, "We've come right in time for the drive-by. Don't worry, no one will hit you."

Their shouts, the whir of the engines, the closeness of the group as we squeeze together—all of it makes me buzz, addicting. When they finally pass and we spread out into the street again, I almost miss them.

"I'm so glad all of you are here," Madison says. "Let's explore a bit, shall we?"

She leads us down the street, her hair suspended like a cloud behind her. To our left, street vendors lean out of their brownstone boutiques and call to us. All the stores resemble Madison's favorite vices: luxury chocolate shops, designer purse boutiques, more shoe shops than I can count. One building simply says, in enormous flashing letters, HAPPY MEMORIES SOLD HERE—a store I'd dreamed up all those years before. The shopkeeper beams as an enormous red parrot hangs off his shoulder.

"Summer vacation!" he yells. "Warm cookies by the fire!

Hugs from your mom! All your best memories, get them right here!"

"Get them right here," the parrot repeats, tilting its head. "Get them right here."

A girl stands near the shopkeeper, watching us file by. A strange sadness twists her expression. She raises one hand, as if in greeting. There's something familiar about her, which only registers when I look away. When I turn back, she's gone.

Devin slips his hand into mine as we go on. "Do you feel that?" he whispers. His pulse throbs against my palm.

"What?"

"The ground," Devin murmurs. "It's breathing."

As soon as he says it, I can feel it. Not just in the ground, but everywhere. This isn't the gray, stern city I visited with my mom. Here, the skyscrapers sigh in and out. The ivy quivers and twitches. Life surges through everything.

I catch my reflection as we pass by a storefront, and nearly fall over. Somehow my avatar looks exactly like me—except better. Usually I try to avoid mirrors, but this time I'm drawn in. All the features are accurate: the tan skin, the mole under my eye, the nervous shape of my mouth. My eyes are still brown, my cheeks still buried under baby fat. Yet somehow the girl in the reflection looks more . . . I don't know. Complete? She's even wearing the same outfit I wore when I walked into the warehouse, a gray V-neck sweater and black jeans, but it's gone from cute to hot. The sweater falls down her shoulder at a perfectly uncareful angle. Her purple hair is freshly dyed, bright all the way up to the roots. She has gentler eyebrows. A new mischief in her grin.

Delight bubbles up in my chest. No wonder everyone is obsessed with this place.

"First things first," Madison calls out. She holds open a door to a clothing shop. "Let's get into appropriate attire."

A surge of confidence sweeps over me. Suddenly I want to pull her aside, ask her what all of this means. I need to hear her say it, that she's made my world real as a way to remember, a way to apologize and reconnect. But she's busy playing host.

We funnel through the door, entering a store that fizzes with purple lighting. Rows of clothing roll out ahead of us, organized by color and arranged into the shape of a rainbow. A chandelier glitters overhead, throwing shards of dazzling color everywhere. A salesman dressed in a tuxedo strides over to us with open arms. Instinctively, I reach toward my pocket, as if shielding my debit card from the sight.

"Free," Madison says as she touches my elbow. She turns to the group. "For those of you who don't know: everything in this city is free. Take what you want. Leave what you want. It. Doesn't. Matter."

Chet and Everly saunter over to the racks, yanking off armloads of clothing. The salesman barks out a laugh, egging us on as the others race after them. Laughter shrieks through the store, the racks rattling. Even Devin lets out a whoop as he disappears into the graphic T-shirt section.

Watching them, I get that lightheaded, bubbly feeling again. I can have anything I want. The bloodred ripped designer jeans. The flowing black gown. The studded boots. *Anything.*

This feels like power. Like arrival.

Madison watches us tear through the shop. She fiddles with one of her simulated piercings. Something about that movement—the subtle uncertainty, her own secret amazement at getting to wear what she wants—softens me. It makes me brave enough to speak.

"This place is amazing, Madison," I say. "It reminds me of our old dream world." I pause, waiting for her to confirm my suspicions. When she stays quiet, I say, "Did you do it on purpose?"

One side of her red mouth tugs up. "I always loved your sketches," she says. "I can't help it. You inspire me."

Giddy warmth blossoms through me. All this time, our school has been obsessed with the world *I* designed. Is this why she never invited me? Was she waiting, testing, fine-tuning so that when I finally arrived, my vision would be perfectly rendered? Or was it something else entirely?

The warmth cools in my chest. I'm flattered, but she should have told me. If her goal was the perfect apology, a strange tribute of sorts, then she made me suffer too much in the meantime. I've spent three years on the outside looking in.

I poke her on the cheek, the way I did in middle school. "If you needed help designing this place, you could have asked."

She pokes me back. "That would've ruined the surprise."

"I wouldn't have cared."

"Let's not do this tonight. Go pick something out."

But I don't want to, yet. I'm just starting to get answers.

"Maybe I like what I'm wearing."

Her eyes finally cut to me. She huffs out a disbelieving laugh. "Everly," she calls. "We need your expertise."

Everly wades out of the racks, sporting enormous yellow sunglasses and an alligator leather bag. She extends one hand.

"Let's go, babe," she says, as if we've been friends for years. "We'll find you the perfect thing."

CHAPTER 8

EVERLY HOLDS UP A BLUE DRESS, THE FABRIC swishing against my shoulder. "Not quite," she says. "It's too much with your purple hair. Let's try something classier."

She leaves and returns with a black tuxedo. I take it from her, the silk material draping elegantly over my hands. It's beautiful in a way I didn't know clothing could be. My nerves light up under it. When I pull it over my shoulders and glance in the mirror, the image I had of myself twists into something new, something sharp and startling. The tux makes me look strong, decisive. Like I could slash a throat and kiss someone senseless in the same breath.

"Too gender-bendy?" Everly asks.

"I don't mind gender-bending," I say. There's a reason I'm dating Devin and not some straight guy. "I actually kind of like it."

Kind of is an understatement. For the first time in my life, I look the way I feel. I'm not trapped in a second-hand uniform or squeezing into one of my mom's old sweaters. I look sharp, queer, artsy. Like the person I want to be.

"And now for the filters," says Everly. "It's like photo editing on HiveMind, but it'll stay on you wherever you go. They have one that's literally just bisexual lighting. It would be perfect with this outfit." She moves her hand in a swiping motion above her head and strikes a pose as moody blue and pink lights glisten across her outfit.

I collapse into laughter. "That is iconic," I say, snorting. "We've got to get Devin in on this. That much bisexual energy in one place could break the simulation."

"You have no idea how hard it was to get Madison's parents to design it," says Everly. "They're not homophobic, they just literally did not understand the *concept* of bisexual lighting. They were like, what do you mean? Do colors have sexualities now?"

My laughter intensifies.

"Now I just need Madison's parents to design some lesbian lighting," Everly says. "Then I'll be unstoppable."

"What would lesbian lighting even be? Pink?"

"Whatever we want it to be," she says.

Everly came out freshman year, around the same time that I did. Madison didn't come out until the year after that. It's funny how queer people find each other before they realize it.

In middle school, I was insanely jealous of Everly. She'd known Madison since preschool, so I couldn't exactly get rid of her. But I shut down Everly's attempts to get closer to me, out of loyalty to Madison. I was secretly delighted when she decided to go out with Mark, because it gave me a reason to hate her. I told myself she was a bad friend, that she didn't deserve Madison. But it was juvenile, jealous shit. Clearly, I lost out on what could've been an incredible friendship.

"Thank you for this." I gesture to the blazer. "I kind of—I don't know. It's been a long time since we hung out."

The dressing room door rattles. Chet's voice slings over to us. "We've got driiiiiiiinks!"

Everly rolls her eyes affectionately. She bumps the door open, revealing Chet in luxury athletic wear. His chest muscles bulge even more than they do in the real world. Behind him, Devin clutches a tray of wineglasses filled to the brim with a pink liquid. He's the hottest dork I've ever seen. Green sweater, khaki pants, confidence radiating off him. Thank God he's having a good time.

"Strawberry lemonade cocktails," Devin announces. "At your service."

"All the alcohol without the hangover. Always buzzed, never drunk." Chet grabs two of the glasses and downs them one after the other.

Everly shoos him away and snatches glasses for us. "You look amazing," she says to Devin, leaning against the open fitting room door.

He laughs. "The store clerk based the outfit on an NPC model called *Brooding Intellectual.* He showed us the designs and everything."

"That model was hot," Chet says. "He makes brooding look like a sexy pastime."

"What do you think?" Devin says to me, spinning around. "Do I look brooding?"

I want to smush his cheeks, and then tackle him with kisses. "Totally brooding," I say. I sip the cocktail and bubbles explode through my mouth like Pop Rocks. As soon as the liquid touches my tongue, the dressing room brightens around me. The overhead disco light splatters through the room like paint. The light blue walls ring into fiercer clarity. How does it feel so real? I guzzle the rest of the cocktail and my senses hike up even further. "Where did Madison go?" I ask Chet.

"Probably went to add some final touches to the party," Everly cuts in. "She's super detail oriented."

"I know," I say without thinking. "She's always been like that."

"Who, me?"

Everly yelps. Devin stumbles backward and nearly drops the wineglasses.

Madison steps out from behind Chet, giggling. "Sorry," she says. "Couldn't resist."

"You nearly gave me a heart attack," Everly hisses.

Madison takes us in, her gaze lingering for a beat longer on me. "You look unreal," she says.

"Like a goddess," Everly agrees. She tucks a loose strand of hair behind my ear, her fingers light as spiders.

I want to lean into their attention, into this feeling of belonging, but a dark feeling spreads underneath my excitement. They've hated me for the last three years and now I'm a goddess? Were they pretending the whole time? Why fix things now?

Somewhere outside the shop, a bell tower clangs. The first hour of the party is already over. As Everly ruffles Devin's hair and Madison leads us back onto the street, I'm struck by the confusing urge to hug them.

Outside, a bloodred sun sinks beneath the skyscrapers. Devin slips his hand into mine as we fall into step with one of the other seniors—the girl from the swim team, Vanessa.

Her dark skin sparkles under the bisexual lighting filter. A white flower crown rests on top of her curly black hair.

"Bree, right?" she says.

My stomach contracts. I almost forgot that I'm still the girl with a drunk dad who nearly killed one of our teachers. Of course she knows me. Everyone knows me.

But then she says, "I think we had English together junior year."

I release a breath and nod. Okay. Yeah.

"Fourth block with Mrs. King, right?"

"Natsby forever," Vanessa says, raising a fist. I laugh. When we read *The Great Gatsby* that year, the class had a forty-five-minute debate on whether there were queer undertones to

Nick and Gatsby's friendship. Which, for the record, there totally were.

I nudge Devin's shoulder. "This is my boyfriend, Devin."

"How do you know Madison?" Devin asks her.

"I don't, really," says Vanessa. "I knew Chet back when he was on the swim team, but we haven't talked much since we—since he quit."

It hits me then, how she got invited. There was rumor that spun through the halls all last winter about Chet and some girl on the swim team. *Vanessa* was that girl. They had a four-month situationship that ended with her cheating on him in the Lincoln pool. Chet dropped out of the team and threatened to beat the shit out of anyone who brought it up.

Before I can respond, Madison's voice seizes our attention. "Everyone hurry up! Over here is Ametrine's Waystation. It's filled with portals to different games."

The crowd follows her into an old-fashioned train station. Giant gilded letters curl over the entrance, reading TRANSPORT YOURSELF ©. Inside, a wide golden ceiling arcs over our heads. Marble angel statues gesture dramatically toward the sky. The room curves around us in a perfect circle, lined with doors that lead to different platforms.

Everly skips over to the door reading PLATFORM ONE. The group watches her, a strange hush falling over the chatter. She grins, savoring our attention. Air-conditioning breezes over us, lifting the hair off the backs of our necks. Everly makes a show of reaching for the gilded door handle, flourishing her arms. Then she pulls it open.

A gust of hot air roars through the door. Devin staggers back, pulling me with him. Yells of shock scatter through the group.

"What *is* that?" someone shrieks.

Scarlet flames rage at the doorframe, hungry, fast, straining to push through. But something holds them at bay, contained to that one room.

Chet bounds forward. "Let's *go*. Fire Battle is back, bitches!"

He's like a dog with the zoomies. He sprints around the room, hooting in victory, pausing every few seconds to shake his ass. The tension dissipates as people laugh at him.

Madison watches Chet with mild amusement. "I don't usually reuse games," she says. "But I had to bring it back, just for you." To the group, she adds, "Last year he loved the game so much that he had an existential crisis. He was like, 'Wait, do I want to be a firefighter? How does someone become a firefighter?'"

Vanessa snorts, but the detail slices into me. Chet—snarky, arrogant, asshole Chet—panicking because he realized he wanted to be a firefighter. It's irritatingly endearing.

"I just wanted to get more pussy," says Chet. "Girls love firefighters."

Ah. There it is.

"Nice," Everly says dryly.

"Sorry, *women* love firefighters."

"Go through the damn portal."

Everly holds open the door and Chet runs, whooping, into the flames. The red swallows him and he disappears. All that's left is the smell of smoke.

"Classy guy," Devin mutters.

Vanessa winces. "Tell me about it."

"All the doors in the Waystation lead to a different VR game," Madison says. "You have one hour here. Go explore!"

Devin glances at me. *Together?*

I nod. *Of course.* Then, feeling Vanessa lingering beside me, I flick my eyes toward her and back to Devin. *Do you think she wants to come with us?*

Before he has the chance to answer, Vanessa points to a door across the room. "That's my lucky number," she says. "Fourteen. Good stuff always happens with the number fourteen. Let's check it out."

Surprise flits through me. I forget sometimes, how easy it can be. For the last three years every attempt at friendship has felt like a strategic battle. A game of cat and mouse, trying to seem busy but not too busy, cool but approachable, down but not desperate. Now that I'm in Ametrine—now that I'm on Madison's good side—it's suddenly easy again.

We follow Vanessa to the fourteenth door and stand back while she swings it open. Wild yellow light streams through, too bright to see what's on the other side.

Vanessa straightens her flower crown and glances back at me. "What do you think?" she asks. "Should we go for it?"

The yellow light shivers, beckoning us in. A giddy feeling bubbles up in my chest. She's asking *me* if I want to go with *her.* For once, a classmate is looking at me with interest. With respect. Like I'm not just some screwed-up alcoholic's daughter. My past shrinks behind me and my present rises up to fill the space. I'm here. I'm *actually* here, in Ametrine, at Madison's party. My acne's gone, my clothes shimmer, and my confidence is growing like a vine. I feel more real, more open, more *me* in Ametrine than I ever did in real life.

I let go of Devin's hand and approach the portal. A chorus of voices croons through the door and I'm drawn in like a sailor to a siren.

"Let's do it," I say, and step through.

Endless sky glistens above us like a blue Jolly Rancher, rippling out in every direction. The air smells sweet enough to drink, the breeze laced with a playful spice. Tall yellow grass reaches up to my waist. It prickles against my pants, and I let myself imagine, for a moment, what I look like from the outside: purple hair, an angular suit, standing alone in a field. For the first time in years, I suspect that I look beautiful.

A soft *zap* behind me, and Devin appears. Vanessa materializes next to him. She covers her mouth with her hand and rotates in a circle, taking in the scene. "This is actually unbelievable," she says. "How did they make it so real?"

Devin runs a thread of wild grass between his fingers. Dried seeds flake off the tip and catch on the breeze, floating off into the sky. He chuckles under his breath and shakes his head in disbelief.

"Greetings," a voice says, and all three of us jump.

A few feet away, a tall white man in a purple cloak stands alone, watching us. He braces his weight on a wooden cane. His eyes linger for a beat too long on me, then move to Devin and Vanessa.

"Um," says Vanessa. "Hi?"

"I have been awaiting your arrival," he says.

A grin spreads over Devin's face. He starts toward the man, but I seize his arm. "What are you doing? We don't know this guy."

"He's an NPC," Devin says. "He must be programmed into the game. God, this is cool. How do you think the Pembrokes created them? Artificial intelligence? Do you think they can learn, or are they stuck repeating certain actions? What if they—"

"He's coming closer," Vanessa says nervously.

She's right. The man strides toward us, robes billowing.

Devin pulls his hair back into a ponytail. A familiar concentration takes over his expression. It's the same look he gets when he plays Dungeons & Dragons. He calls out to the stranger as he approaches us. "What is your name, good sir?"

The old man pauses. He leans on his cane, considering the question. Devin waits, a new confidence straightening his shoulders. God, I love this side of him.

"I am no one," the old man says, bowing his head. "And everyone."

Vanessa busts out laughing. "What is this?" she says. "Some kind of role-playing game?"

"This is no game," says the man.

Vanessa shoots me a skeptical look. The man lazily raises one hand. Devin clocks the movement. He lurches forward and shouts, "*Wait!*" but by then Vanessa is already screaming. The grass at her feet snarls around her legs, tying her in place.

"Dude!" Vanessa yelps. "Not cool!"

I jump to her side and try to tear the grass free, but it's locked around her legs, digging deep enough to cut the skin. The blades crawl farther up her legs, weaving around her waist.

He isn't playing around.

"You dare disrespect me?" the old man (the old . . . wizard?) bellows. He brandishes his cane.

Devin moves toward him, pressing his hands together as if in prayer. "Good sir, please forgive my companion. We are mere travelers in this strange land, and we are not yet accustomed to your—"

"Silence!" He points his cane straight at Devin's face. "The only way to resolve such an offense is a duel. To the death."

Devin doesn't cower from the cane, hovering inches from his nose. He nods solemnly. Vanessa starts giggling again, then breaks off when the grass tightens around her. A flash of embarrassment heats my face. To me, Devin's seriousness is cute as hell. But what does Vanessa think? Does he look like a loser through her eyes?

"Very well," Devin says.

"Your power lies in your hands," says the old man. "You must flex your right thumb, like so, to release your—"

A lightning bolt erupts from Devin's fist. It whizzes through the air and smashes straight into the old man, knocking him over in a flurry of robes.

"Oh shit!" Vanessa shrieks.

The man howls in rage. Devin hits him with another lightning strike, then another.

I try to mimic what Devin's doing by flexing my thumb into my palm. Long, sharp blades hiss out of my knuckles, Wolverine-style. Not as cool as lightning, but—Vanessa thrashes and yanks at the grass—just as useful.

I kneel at Vanessa's side and slash at her restraints. The grass shrinks back, flinching under the attack. Behind me, the wizard tosses spells at Devin.

Vanessa tears the last piece of grass off her leg, panting.

"Thank God," she says. A smile breaks across her face as she nods toward Devin. "Damn, look at him go."

Devin aims crack after crack of lightning. Each shot makes perfect impact, the sound thundering through the field. Devin's face glows wild and exquisite with power.

I turn back to Vanessa, but she's disappeared. I whirl around in a circle, alarmed. Then she reappears, fast as a blink. She wiggles her fingers.

"Apparently I can turn invisible," she says. She stretches her arms over her head, as if warming up for exercise. Then, to my infinite delight, she puts on an overly serious British accent. "I started this. Now I must finish it."

She disappears.

A shocked laugh shakes my body. Up ahead, the wizard stops fighting, succumbing to Devin's attacks. He careens to the ground, waving the cane in front of himself. But then, somehow, the cane disappears from the wizard's grip. Devin pauses, confused.

Vanessa appears several feet away with a wicked smile, raising the cane above her head.

"Die!" she says, and aims a final blast.

The wizard lets out a bloodcurdling screech. The spell launches into his chest, and he explodes into a ball of silver light. Dramatic orchestral music swells around us, underscoring the importance of this moment. A battle won, a level cleared. When the smoke dissipates, the wizard is gone. All that's left is a scorched mark in the grass.

Devin whoops. Vanessa runs over and high-fives him. I double over with laughter as they do a ridiculous victory dance together. Devin shoots lightning bolts into the sky, shaking his hips with exaggerated swagger. Vanessa flickers in and out of visibility like a strobe light. We're still celebrating when a new voice interrupts.

"Madison's looking for you."

Kyle stands a few feet away with his hands in his pockets. When did he get here?

Devin and Vanessa stop dancing. Vanessa tilts her head. "Has it been an hour already?" she asks.

Kyle shrugs, avoiding our eyes. He jerks his head toward a golden door that hovers behind him—a door that I hadn't noticed until now, but must be the one we came through.

"Come on," he says, and we follow.

Outside the Waystation, Kyle directs the crowd of rowdy partygoers into a line. Elbows jostle and we peer over each other's shoulders to get a glimpse of what we're waiting for. At the front of the line, Kyle kneels down in the street next to a circular sewer grate.

"What the hell?" murmurs a freshman near me.

Kyle hooks his fingers into the grate, twists, and lifts it free with a metallic pop. He stands back and Mark saunters over, clearly familiar with this ritual. He approaches the sewer, turns back to the crowd, and winks. Then he leaps straight into the hole and disappears.

Gasps burst over the group. Mark's triumphant yell echoes up out of the ground. Madison studies her nails, mouth twitching like she's trying not to smile.

Everly twirls over to the sewer grate, curtsies, and jumps in after Mark. One by one, the invitees approach and descend. Some crawl in carefully, lowering themselves inch by inch before dropping. Others feign confidence, cannonballing or diving in headfirst. Devin and I are the last to go. We linger next to Kyle, hanging on to each second that we have left.

"The role-playing game was more fun," says Devin. "This is kind of stressing me out."

Kyle offers a weird, forced smile. He points to the sewer. Devin sighs. He kisses me on the head and sits down so his legs dangle into the hole. "See you," he says, and pushes himself in.

As soon as Devin's gone, I jump.

Darkness rushes around me like water. It sucks at my skin, tangles in my hair. It floods my mouth with the taste of salt. Then my back collides with a trampoline and I soar up, down again, up—and lights break over me like a final ocean wave. I settle on the trampoline and twist around, trying to get my bearings.

EDM thunders through the air. Above me, the sewer tunnel extends up in a long glass line. In fact, everything around me is made of glass. The floor beneath the trampoline, the walls surrounding me—and behind that glass, an ocean teeming with aquatic creatures. A shark glides by, its wide mouth gaping open.

A hand grips my elbow, pulls me off the trampoline and into a crush of people. Madison registers in front of me, then Devin, then Vanessa.

Everly shoves a drink in my hand. Gummy sharks float in the blue liquid.

"Welcome to the Abyss," Madison says as her pearly laugh churns in the air.

The underwater nightclub—another design plucked from our childhood fantasies. I'd based it off the Boston aquarium that we visited with Grandma Edie. But here, strobe lights puncture my vision. Music pounds out in every direction. NPCs press up against us, countless virtual bodies grinding to the beat.

Nearby, one girl stands without moving, staring at us. The crowd bends and dances around her. My stomach twinges in discomfort. Why is she looking at us like that?

"Who is that?" I ask Madison, gesturing to the girl.

Madison looks up from her watch. "Who?"

I point, but the girl is gone. A chill goes up my back.

Madison wears an amused expression. "You've got to see the VIP room," she yells over the music. "Come with me."

Devin covers his ears with his hands. "Do we have to? It's so loud."

"It's quieter up there," says Madison. "Let's go."

Devin looks to me, uncertain. "Bree, something feels off."

"What do you mean?"

"I just—" Sweat shines on his forehead. "It was fun before. But this part of the simulation is kind of overstimulating. I think I need to take a break."

My stomach jolts. I'd almost forgotten we were even *in* a VR. I raise my hands in front of me, and for a second I can't match up the motion with my real hands, the ones still in a console. I bite down the flare of panic.

"Motion sickness is super normal in the beginning. It'll pass," says Madison. She tugs me forward. "Let's go. I want to show you more of our world."

Her pupils are wide enough to swallow me, two blackened moons. The Madison I knew feels close, straining under her surface. That confident smirk. Her hand, cold in mine.

"It'll be fine," I say to Devin. "You'll feel better upstairs."

Madison's smile widens. She leads me through the chaos, to whatever waits beyond.

CHAPTER 9

MADISON TAKES US TO A GLASS ELEVATOR. THE doors hiss shut, blocking out the party. For the moment it's only the three of us, surrounded by water.

Madison twists at her smart watch, and the elevator shoots up. My ears pop. I finish the dregs of my drink and try to muscle through the awkward silence. Madison watches Devin closely, but he doesn't meet her eyes.

"It's so crazy that we haven't hung out before," she says to him.

Devin's eyebrows pull down, not quite into a grimace. "It's not that crazy. You've made Bree's life hell."

"Devin," I mutter. "Not now."

"No, it's okay. I get it." Madison taps the glass and sighs. "I know I haven't been there for you, Bree. But I'm hoping we can get some closure tonight. Start over, you know?"

Annoyance flits through me—it's so typical that she gets to choose when and how we make up. She always wants to make the rules, to assert her dominance and *win*. But no matter how frustrating that is, another part of me is relieved. At this point, I just want all the tension to be over.

The elevator eases to a halt. Music draws us like a riptide into the VIP room.

About half a dozen partygoers are there, sipping cocktails on a gilded sofa, gossiping, dancing. No NPCs. Devin squints against the flashing blue lights.

Everly dances over to me, carrying more neon drinks. "God, I love this song!" She passes me the concoction. I gulp down the drink and the simulation brightens, widens. A pleasant heat coats my body. "Dance with me!" she says.

"I'm going to go sit down," Devin says.

"I'll meet you over there," I promise, kissing his cheek. Then I fall into step with Everly, my self-consciousness burning away.

The music guides my limbs, vibrates through my spine. Bodies blur around me. I haven't danced like this since I was a kid—since I wore shirts with sparkly peace signs and rocked out with Madison in her garage. Arms out, hips swaying. Belting songs I don't even know the words to. I can feel Madison's eyes on me, but I'm too buzzed to care. Another drink, then another. Laughter spasms through my chest. The world tilts in and out of focus. Mark grooves over, catches me mid-twirl, and dips me like a princess. We'd danced like this back in eighth grade, a lifetime ago. He's so much taller now. That's the power of Ametrine: we haven't spoken for years, and now he's spinning me in circles in front of everyone.

Chet whoops from the sofa. He drapes one arm over Madison as she sits down beside him. She taps her smart watch. The lights and music cool off.

"Everyone over here," she says.

I wipe a thread of sweat off my forehead as the dancing winds down. Everly corrals us toward Madison, into a circle around her couch. I find Devin sitting on the floor and ruffle his hair before sinking down beside him.

"You looked beautiful dancing," he murmurs in my ear.

"Not enough room?" says Madison. She adjusts something on her watch and an enormous waterbed couch materializes under us. Sounds of appreciation flit across the group as we settle in, startled fish darting around beneath the plastic mattress.

It's insane that Madison can just . . . do that. A flick of the wrist, and she remakes reality around us.

Everly sits down on my right, and Vanessa settles in next to Devin. Across from us, a vaguely familiar sophomore sits with his legs sprawled out.

Vanessa leans over to me. "Is that Jake Brown?"

The kid who left Ametrine after only five minutes? How the hell did he score another invite? Everyone assumed he was done for.

Madison plucks Chet's arm off her shoulder. She hops up onto the arm of the couch, perching like a bird. "You all know I love games," she says. "Since it's a party, I say we bring back a classic: Never Have I Ever."

She taps her watch, and the overhead lights change again, zapping into scarlet lines. A heart monitor appears over each person's head, a line graph twitching up and down with our heartbeats.

"I've activated a truth filter over the room," says Madison. "It monitors your heart rate and body temperature, and tells us when you're lying. There will be consequences for anyone who tries to get around it."

In unison, everyone's heart graph ticks up, prompting a wave of nervous giggles. Everly and Chet exchange glances.

Consequences. I wonder what Madison means. In middle school, she forced rule-breakers to take shots of a nasty sludge she made from toothpaste and ice cream.

"I'll go first," Madison says. "Never have I ever cheated on a test."

About half of the room drinks. Devin doesn't, and neither do I.

"Nerds of honor," he says, grinning at me. We clink glasses.

The graphs twitch over our heads, then stabilize. No liars this time.

"One time," Everly says. "*Once.* My parents would have killed me if I got a B."

"It's easy to cheat on Zoom exams," Jake says.

Chet raises his glass in solidarity with the other cheaters. "Not sorry about it."

"Your turn," Madison says to him.

Chet's eyes move lazily across the room and stop on Vanessa. "Never have I ever . . ." He pauses, soaking in the drama. "Hooked up with someone in the Lincoln pool."

Vanessa barks out a laugh beside me. "You've got to be kidding me."

Chet doesn't flinch. Everyone stares, waiting for her to confirm the rumor.

She takes a swig and wipes her mouth. "Okay, so we're playing personal," she says. Her voice stays light, good-natured. "Game on. Never have I ever . . . had a crush on Madison Pembroke."

Chet's eyes narrow to slits. His heart rate flares up as he leans back and crosses his arms. Then, to no one's surprise, he drains his cocktail glass.

Everly leans over to me as gossip crackles around the room. "Take a drink," she whispers.

"What?" I force a laugh. My heartbeat thrums in my palms, and I feel Devin watching me. "I don't have a crush on Madison."

"The question was if you've *ever* had a crush on her," Everly says. The crowd's attention stays on Madison as she pats Chet's head.

Devin nudges me. "Hey, it's okay. A lot of queer friendships are like that."

My fingers feel locked into place. I force myself to keep smiling, like this whole thing is ridiculous. "I've never had a crush on her," I whisper back. "We were just friends."

Friends who spent literally every second together. Friends who valued loyalty above all else. Friends who didn't know they were queer yet.

Shit.

"Your graph is going crazy," Everly insists. I notice, suddenly, that she's taken a drink too. "Drink, now, or you're gonna be—"

"Uh-oh," says Madison, her attention falling on Evan, a junior from our AP Calculus class. "Do we have a liar?"

The graph over his head dings and flashes. I swallow my pride and sneak a drink while no one's watching. Madison rises to her feet and circles over to Evan, her silver hair rippling. She slides a hand under his chin and tilts his face so he looks up at her. "Why lie?" she says softly. "It's nothing to be embarrassed about."

"This thing is broken," Evan says. "You're hot, for sure. But dating you would be like dating a shark. I'm not trying to get my head bit off."

"So sweet," she says, patting his cheek. She turns away from him, darkness twisting over her expression. "And such a waste. I hate to see guests get thrown out of Ametrine so soon."

She taps her watch.

Evan glitches. His image fractures in half, then into thirds. A scream barely works its way out of his mouth—then he disappears, exiled from Ametrine.

Madison turns back to the crowd. "Now, do you all understand the rules?"

CHAPTER 10

NO LYING. NINE PEOPLE. AND A PARTY GAME.

The players: Madison, the ringleader. Everly, her sidekick, chewing her nails to stubs. Chet and Vanessa, whose questions have become increasingly pointed. Kyle, who keeps his mouth shut. Jake, who doesn't. Mark, Devin, and me.

"Never have I ever waxed my chest," says Vanessa.

Chet rolls his eyes and drinks. "Never have I ever gone to homecoming alone," he says.

Jake shrieks with glee. His eyebrows pinch downward, giving him a permanently mean look.

"Never have I ever sent an ugly dick pic," Vanessa says.

"Never have I ever eaten lunch alone in the library," Chet hits back.

"Never have I ever gotten a boner during a swim meet!"

"Never have I ever been abandoned by my own *mother*!"

Everyone freezes. Madison's jaw drops open in delight. Vanessa looks like he slapped her in the face. She opens her mouth, then closes it, speechless.

"Whoa," Kyle says, breaking in for the first time. "Hold on. That's—"

"Jesus Christ," Everly mutters under her breath. "How does he even know that?"

Angry tears shine in Vanessa's eyes. She stares at her knees, the muscles in her jaw jumping. The graph flashes over her head as her heart rate escalates. I want to reach for her, to protect her somehow, but I suspect it would only embarrass her more.

Kyle's high voice wobbles. "That's too far, Chet. You shouldn't—"

"Oh?" Chet cracks his knuckles one at a time. "Okay. Thanks for your opinion, Kyle. Let's do another one. Never have I ever peed my pants in high school."

The color leaches out of Kyle's face. He lowers his eyes and takes a drink.

"You're kidding!" Jake points at Kyle, shaking with laughter. "Holy shit, that is disgusting. When? When did that happen?"

"Would you leave him alone?" Vanessa glares at him. "Never have I ever been the shortest person in this room."

Jake's laughter halts. He surveys the group, disbelieving, then takes a grudging sip. Madison leans back in her seat, eyes glinting. Is she actually enjoying this?

Devin looks like he wants to throw himself out a window. I rub his shoulder, worry gnawing through me. What is this bringing up for him? Is he reliving the bullying at his old school? We need to change course, fast.

Chet returns to his attack on Vanessa. "Never have I ever lied about being a virgin for attention."

"Can we stop?" I say. I shoot Madison a pleading expression. "This isn't fun anymore."

Madison tilts her head. "Okay," she says. "I have one that will make this more fun." She trails her finger down Chet's arm. "Never have I ever . . . fantasized about hooking up with the math teacher."

Heat rushes to my face. It sprouts up my neck, cuts between my eyes. The graph wails over my head, giving me away to everyone. Dr. Leon. How did she—

"You're incredibly obvious," Madison says, as I take a humiliating drink. "All those extra questions after class . . . Honestly, it's kind of hard to watch."

"*Dr. Leon?*" Chet snorts. "You must have a nerd kink. What does Devvy think?"

"Leave her alone," says Devin, voice rising. "I don't care about that shit."

I know he doesn't want me to stoop to their level. But facing Madison—staring into that arrogant dimple on her cheek—something hardens in me. She wants to play dirty? Fine. I reach into my memories and pull out a weapon.

"Never have I ever cried over my parents bailing on a dance recital," I say.

Madison goes still. The memory weaves between us: age

eleven, in matching purple leotards, performing in *The Nutcracker.* Madison had scrambled through the dark auditorium afterward, looking for her parents, her small face lit up with hope—and found no one. Yet another event her parents skipped for a last-minute work meeting. She cried in the bathroom for ten minutes straight after that, wrecking her stage makeup. That night, my parents were the ones to drive her home.

Now her gaze stays locked on mine as her truth filter goes haywire. Laughter shatters through the crowd.

"Poor little princess!" Everly says.

"I can picture the exact fucking look on her face," Chet says. "You were such a brat."

Devin shakes his head in disbelief. I know he's disappointed in me, but the guilt barely registers—it feels good, putting Madison in her place. Reminding her of the power that I have.

Her expression stays blank as she watches me. There was a time when I could read every twitch of her cheek, translate each blink, every micro-emotion. Not anymore. I have no idea what she's thinking. A flash of fear hits me. Is she going to kick me out of Ametrine? I don't want to leave yet. The night's barely started. But bringing up her parents in front of everyone . . . I don't know what she'll do.

"Drink! Drink! Drink!" Jake says.

Red lights careen above Madison's chart. She glances sideways at Mark, and her heart rate monitor speeds up even faster.

"Go on," I say.

The rest of the room joins in: "Drink! Drink! Drink!"

She raises her cocktail glass and downs the whole thing. Blue liquid runs down her chin, beads on her neck. Then, with a swipe of her watch, she removes the truth filter and stands up.

"I'm bored," she says, voice husky. "I think it's time to raise the stakes."

CHAPTER 11

OUTSIDE, DARKNESS FILLS THE STREET, SPILLING LIKE INK in water.

I don't remember leaving the club—one moment I'm sitting on the couch next to Vanessa, the next I'm swaying on my feet in an unfamiliar alley. Long, twisting buildings glare down at us from both sides. I rub my eyes, try to regain some focus. What was in those drinks? Whatever it was, it makes the brightness brighter and the darkness darker. I wish I could bring these colors back home with me, contort them into a collage. There are so many pieces of this world that I want to use. The effervescent blue of our cocktails. A square of fabric from my suit. But mostly, I want to feel centered again.

Shadows smudge the people around me into outlines. Nausea pumps through my stomach. I reach to my left, feeling for Devin's hand, and find only empty air.

"Devin?" I call out.

No response.

The darkness closes in on me, claustrophobic. "*Devin?*" I shout. "Where—"

"Truth or Dare," says Madison, from across the street.

I startle, breath catching. She stands with her back straight, bathed in a silver spotlight, ghostlike. Though I hear breathing around me, she is the only person I can see clearly. Why are there no streetlights? And why did she bring us here?

"Where's Devin?" I ask her. "He was beside me when we left."

"Not so tough without him, are you?" she says.

"What?" I rub my eyes, disoriented. The brief sense of power I had drains away. "You're being—that's—can you stop? Please? Seriously. Where is he?"

She just smiles. Terror swells through me.

"This isn't funny." My voice shakes. "I don't want to be here without him. Tell me where he is."

"Play the game," she says, "and I'll show you."

My heart slams in my chest. I'm tempted to yank off this headset, to get the hell out of here, but—I came this far. And I won't leave Devin behind. Who knows what they have planned? He'd be completely alone, at Madison's mercy.

"Mark," says Madison. "You can go first."

At the sound of his name, a light grows around Mark too. The silver distorts his skin tone, makes him look pale and sickly. But he's grinning that familiar easy grin, stretching his arms gamely when he says, "Dare."

Madison points to the building behind him. "Climb it."

"All the way up?" says Vanessa's voice, high with concern. "In the dark?"

"No prob," says Mark, strolling over. He places his hand against the wall and leans in, as if listening for a heartbeat. He rips a handful of ivy off the wall and examines it. Then he removes his blazer and hands it to me. He brushes his hands on his pants, jogs in place a little. His shoulder muscles flex as he reaches up and hoists himself up over the door.

The partygoers draw together in the street as he ascends the building. My elbow brushes against Jake. He's a mouth breather, going "Oh, *oh*!" with barely contained joy whenever Mark hesitates in the climb.

Mark makes it to the top freakishly fast. I can't help but wonder if Madison gave him an advantage, knowing how athletic he is. She snaps her fingers and he teleports back to the ground, dizzy with triumph.

"Very nice," she says. "Mark, you choose someone now."

I hand back his blazer. He folds it over one arm and singles out the sophomore. "You," he says. "Jake, right?"

"Yeah, that's him," Chet says. "The wuss from last year."

"Truth or dare?" Mark says.

"Truth."

"How many times a day do you jerk off?"

Madison lets out a shriek of laughter and activates a truth filter over Jake's head. Jake opens his mouth, then closes it. Color rises in his cheeks.

"You have to answer," Chet says.

"Twice." Jake crosses his arms, tries to play off his embarrassment. "Sometimes three times."

Laughter echoes down the street, bounces off the buildings. Vanessa, all snorts and cackles. Everly, almost musical in her mirth. Even I can't help but smile—it's alarmingly easy to enjoy his embarrassment. He shoves his hand through his hair and turns to me.

"Truth or dare?"

Shit.

I want to leave, find Devin, go back to dancing, shopping. But Madison is in control here, with that smart watch, and—there is no way I am telling any of them about my masturbation habits.

"Dare," I say.

Madison leans over and whispers something into Jake's ear. He cackles and kneels down to pick something off the ground. As the light moves from his face to mine, it illuminates a long, black cockroach dangling from his fingers.

"I dare you to eat it," he says.

Queasiness rolls up my stomach. The cockroach strains against the sophomore's hand, its tiny legs contracting and expanding.

"Ugh. Seriously?"

"Don't be scared," Madison says. "I figured this should remind you of home."

Blood pounds in my face as I turn to her. "Excuse me?"

"You know," Madison says, nodding to the cockroach. "Since you changed neighborhoods."

Rage tightens my skin, sends waves of heat through my body. We look at each other, sizing each other up. I'd forgotten about this feeling until now. The two of us, locked in competition, trying to one-up each other in front of our friends. Underhanded compliments. Loaded questions. Shitty comments we'd hold against each other for weeks, dancing between guilt and revenge. My skin itches as more memories surface. We were best friends, but it wasn't all sweetness. There had always been an unspoken rivalry between us. In a weird way, that rivalry had made us even closer.

Suspicion flares up in me. Why did she actually invite me here? Does she really want to make up, or is this a final strategic move in a yearslong game?

Then, another question, this one more alarming because somehow I didn't even consider it—I mean truly, fully consider it—until now: do *I* still want to be friends with *her*?

This side of her isn't new. It's easy to forget, in the drought of loneliness, in the glaze of memories. But we were not kind to each other. At least, not all the time. She brought out an ugly side of me. And now here she is, talking shit in front of our classmates, making me feel pathetic again. Does she really think this is the way to forgiveness?

Madison's eyes glint. There's a challenge in her expression, an invitation. With Devin gone, she's baiting me into our old game. *You hurt me, I hurt you.*

The cockroach gleams in Jake's fingers. She thinks I won't do it. That I'm too weak, too sensitive. But she doesn't know me anymore.

"Do it, Bree," Chet says. "Don't be a pussy."

"Pussy is a lazy insult," Vanessa says.

"Bill Gates says laziness is a sign of intelligence," Chet retorts. "Lazy people find quicker solutions. Don't be a pussy, Bree."

"You chose dare," Madison says softly, eyes on me. "Now see it through."

This is her last party. After tonight, a significant amount of her social leverage is gone. If I play this right, maybe it doesn't matter if I forgive her. Maybe some of her friends would rather hang with me.

It's not real, I remind myself as I take the roach, as I pinch it between my fingers. *This isn't my real body. This isn't my real mouth. It's a haptic suit, messing with my brain.* The black shiny eyes drill through me. Its flaky wing beats against my thumb. *Just play the game and get to Devin. Fast.*

I hold it between my lips and bite in. Its body spasms under my teeth, a taste like mildew cracking through my mouth. Bile clogs my throat, but I force myself to swallow, first one half, then the other. I gag, cover my mouth, manage to keep it down. Barely.

Everly and Vanessa cheer. Kyle holds his stomach, grimacing. I need to get the spotlight off myself, like right now, so I turn to him. "Truth or dare?"

He releases his stomach and looks up at me, his expression queasy. "Truth," he says.

If I were to infiltrate and break down Madison's social group—not that I want to, but if I did—Kyle would be an easy starting point. He's on the outer flank of her group, never quite fitting in with the others. He's so anxious and insecure that I suspect that any kindness would melt him.

So I ask him a genuine question, one that I think he'd like to answer. "Why didn't you audition for the musical this year?"

It's supposed to be easy. His parents weren't supportive, or his schedule got too busy. But at the question, his face closes up. He gets this frightened animal look, where I can see the whites of his eyes, and he keeps glancing at Madison, as if she knows the answer. He shakes his head, opens his mouth like he's going to speak, then Chet butts in before he can answer.

"Lame," he says. "I have a better one. Vanessa, truth or dare?"

"Wow, you are obsessed with me," she says. The light snaps from Kyle to her. Her eyes twinkle. "Dare."

"Go for a swim," Chet says.

"What?"

"Madison?" he says.

Madison taps her watch. Air rips around us, the world

sears sheet-white, then suddenly we're standing on a rocky cliffside, water buffeting against the shore twenty feet below.

I stumble, manage not to fall. Vanessa grabs my arm, wincing. Can Madison teleport any player, whenever she wants? She can banish people, change the way they look, force them to tell the truth . . . but the enormity of her power still won't sink in. What else can she do?

At school, she's a queen bee, a billionaire in waiting.

In Ametrine, she's a *god*.

The air has a slimy, saline flavor. A hooked crescent moon dangles overhead. It's bright enough that we can finally see each other without the migrating glow. Vanessa peers over the edge of the cliff. The wine-colored water seethes and tosses.

"You still scared of sharks?" Chet asks her.

"Maybe in real life," Vanessa says. She removes her flower crown, then her shoes. She keeps on her white dress, the frills battering against her thighs. "If you're trying to freak me out, you'll have to try a little harder." She backs up, her movement fast and liquid. My jaw aches from clenching.

When she turns to face us, she gives Chet a little salute. Then she launches into a backward dive, her legs spiraling up over her head, and she shoots out over the cliff. She seems to fall for hours, her white dress a scar against the blackness, then her arms catch the water and she slings under, pitch-perfect.

I cheer with my hands cupped around my mouth. Holy

shit, she's amazing. I've never seen her dive before. Jake joins in cheering, but Everly and Madison stay quiet. Chet leans over and watches. It's like they're all waiting for something.

Vanessa waves up at us. Lead-colored clouds boil overhead.

A shadow passes under her. Vanessa flinches, looking around as she treads water. The shadow races by again, and ripples spread out at an unnatural angle—the water moved by something other than Vanessa's arms.

Thunder growls above us. Vanessa shouts something, but her voice is lost in the growing wind. Then fins begin to circle.

A gasp lodges in my windpipe.

Chet nods toward the sharks. His voice is indifferent, but his eyes never waver from Vanessa. "Would you look at that."

She takes off for the shore, her arms cutting through the waves. The fins multiply, a horde of sharks streaking behind her. A scream shatters up the rocks and then she's frozen, sinking, her hands reaching out for something to hold on to.

Jake seizes my shoulder. The screams swell louder, choked with water as she slips below the surface.

Madison snaps her fingers and Vanessa teleports back to us, soaked to her skin, hair splayed out across her face. She falls on her hands and knees, convulsing with sobs. I run to her side, try to help her to her feet, but she jerks away. She clutches her chest, hyperventilating—then lurches down and vomits. Bile glistens in the dirt. "I almost drowned," she says. "I—I couldn't breathe, I—"

I say her name, but it's like she can't hear me. Sobs spasm through her, so physical that she looks possessed. She retches again and again, wheezing.

"Something wrong?" Chet says, standing over her.

"You're an asshole," she spits.

"You seem pretty freaked out," he says. "Hope you're not afraid of water now. It would really mess up your swimming scholarship if you couldn't actually swim."

Vanessa turns to Madison, clambers to her feet. "I'm done. Get me the fuck out of here."

"Don't go," I butt in. It's selfish, I know, but if she leaves, it's only me and Jake against Madison's inner circle.

Madison slinks toward Vanessa. "What, are you scared of a little fun?"

She's gone sweet again, wearing the same innocence that she did with me in the elevator. *You inspire me,* she'd said. *Tonight, we're starting over.*

Water drips down Vanessa's hair, soaks her clothes. She looks past Madison to Chet. "You've had your fun with me," she says.

She raises her hands to her temples, to where her goggles would be in real life. And then her body slumps to the ground, unconscious.

CHAPTER 12

MADISON AIMS A KICK AT VANESSA'S LIFELESS BODY. "God, that is so annoying."

"What the *fuck*?" I fall to my knees, shake Vanessa's shoulders. Her eyes roll back, unseeing. "What did you do?"

"She did it herself," says Everly. "When you quit early, you leave your avatar behind. Madison, when are your parents going to fix that?"

"I'll take care of it," Madison mutters. She taps her watch a few times, and Vanessa's body disappears. Then she brushes her hands together, as if finishing a messy job. "What a buzzkill. Let's get out of here."

She teleports us again—this time to a gothic version of our elementary school playground. It has all the same equipment, but everything here breathes violence. The monkey bars are lined with razor-sharp spikes. A dark liquid pools at the bottom of the slide. Curved streetlights guard the schoolyard, bathe us in a color like yellowed teeth. It's our old home, made haunted.

I have no idea how to get back to the Abyss, no idea how to

return to Devin and the other partygoers. And now that Vanessa's gone, I don't trust anyone here to help me find out. Kyle's completely shut down. Jake will do anything Madison says, desperate to redeem himself from last year. Chet is . . . Chet. And it's not like I can pull Everly to my side.

My suit feels too tight, the air tense and close. Shit. Shit. *Shit.*

No, okay. Deep breaths. I can figure this out. The party always lasts exactly twelve hours. I heard the bell tower go off at the clothing shop, and it's been at least a couple of hours since then. So I have, what? Nine hours left? Eight? Oh, God. Eight hours. She won't keep us separated from the group for all that time. Right? Dread razes over my skin. What's happening in my haptic suit to make me feel like this? How does this VR world even work?

Madison directs us to sit down, and I force myself to obey. We lower ourselves into a circle on the pricking brown grass, under one of the streetlamps. Mark sits on my left, Jake on my right.

"Too bad about the swim girl," says Everly. As if she's too cool to remember her name.

Madison shrugs. "Not everyone has what it takes."

But why should Vanessa have to prove herself? It's supposed to be a party, not a test, and that shark dare was fucked-up. I think of her face, fresh out of the water, how she grabbed at her chest as though she were dying. Kyle's terror when I asked about the musical. I study Madison's face, trying to understand. What is she doing? Why is any of this necessary?

And why can't I shake the feeling that somehow, all of it has to do with me?

"Whose turn is it?" Chet asks, picking his teeth.

"Mine," says Madison. She leans forward, toward Jake. "Truth or dare?"

Jake sits with his legs splayed out, overly comfortable as usual. He yawns, as if this whole thing bores him. "Dare."

Madison scans him up and down. She reaches out and takes one of his hands. He leans into the touch. "This is a nice ring," she says. She traces her finger over the gold band on his pinky finger. "Give it to me."

Jake raises an eyebrow. He twists at the ring, but Madison stops him.

"Not like that," she says. She snatches at the air, summoning a long, hooked knife.

I choke down a gasp. Mark stiffens beside me.

She leans over to Jake, offering him the blade. A smile wanders up her mouth. "I want the finger too."

Chet whoops, startling a murder of crows. Their dark wings slash overhead as they erupt into the air. "You sick fuck!" he says delightedly.

Everly giggles into her palm, a high nervous sound. Madison's focus stays on the sophomore, her smile sharper than the weapon, the dare hovering between them. "You begged for another chance in Ametrine," she says. "You said you'd do anything."

What. The. Fuck. I knew Madison had a dark side, but this is insane, even for her.

"You don't have to do this," I blurt out.

"Yeah," Chet says, voice bright. "You could always pussy out, like last time. Then we can finish telling everyone how pathetic you are."

Jake accepts the knife. His tongue flicks out, wets his lip as he looks around the group.

"Jake," I say. "Seriously—"

"My hand in the real world will be fine?" he says.

"Sure," Madison says. "But you'll still feel it, for as long as you're in the simulation."

Kyle's hands tremble in his lap. Jake holds Madison's gaze. Neither of them backs down.

I fold and unfold my legs underneath me, pants itching against the grass. It's like watching a horror movie, the part where a character descends into the creepy basement and you want to throw popcorn at the screen, yell at them to *get out, you idiot!*

"That's eight hours," Mark says, after a moment. "You'd just have to make it that long."

"Or," Everly says, "like Chet said, you're welcome to go home, and miss the rest of the party."

“Can’t you heal it?” Jake says to Madison. “Once I cut it off?”

“Maybe,” Madison says. “If I decide you deserve it.”

What is she doing? There’s nothing recognizable in this version of Madison. It’s like she’s playing a character, one of the hot villains she imprinted on as a kid, someone who draws their power from cruelty. This is the same girl who full-body sobbed when Robert Gray killed a spider during recess. Now she’s making some poor kid amputate his own finger?

Still, I stay quiet. He won’t listen, and I need to survive this night as much as anyone else does. I need to get to wherever Devin is, to stay long enough to find him and tell him what’s going on. He was right about Madison and her friends. He was right about everything.

It’s not real. Remember it’s not real.

Jake lines the knife up against his pinky. He lifts the handle and points the tip into the dirt in front of his knuckle, like lining up a cucumber.

Chet’s eyes gleam. Everly covers her face with her hands.

I squeeze my eyes shut, turn my face away.

Thwunk.

His screams shatter through the playground. Crows circle overhead, cawing. Hysterical laughter spins around us, Chet and Everly collapsing onto each other. Jake cradles his hand, curses streaming out between sobs. Blood gushes from his hand in floods of scarlet, white bone jutting out. Kyle gags, covering his mouth with his hand. The knife glistens at their feet.

Madison and I are the only ones not laughing. I can't alchemize my horror fast enough, can't pretend to enjoy this.

"Madison," Jake gasps. "Please. I did it—now heal me—"

She ignores him and turns to me. "Your turn."

Her attention feels like a physical weight bearing down onto my shoulders. Next to me, Jake is screaming, blood everywhere, tears and snot speckling his face, and she doesn't even look over.

"*Madison.* Please! You said you'd heal me. My hand—please, fuck, it hurts—*please*—"

"Bree," she says. "Truth or dare?"

"You need to help him," I say.

Her eyes narrow. Jake hunches over his hand, wailing. Chet picks up the amputated finger and waves it triumphantly in the air.

"I'll help him when you answer," she says.

"What? Why? Madison, he's in pain! What are you—"

"He can leave if he wants to," she says. "Now answer. Truth or dare?"

Kyle and Mark wrap a scarf around Jake's hand. Kyle rubs his back and murmurs something in his ear. Chet throws the severed finger up and down, like he does with his pencil.

"Truth," I say, voice shaking.

"I've heard the craziest rumor." Sugar infects her tone, makes the hairs on my arms rise up. "About you and Paul Rodgers."

Oh, God. Not Paul Rodgers.

So, okay. We went out to the movies once (One time. Once!) during eighth grade. Madison set up the date, played matchmaker, got us two seats at *Jeepers Creepers: Reborn.* Paul and I held hands for a while, my palms wet with popcorn grease, then he guided my hand into his lap, under his navy-blue rain jacket, and—

"Is it true you gave him a hand job at the movie theater?"

Look, it's not my proudest moment.

"In my defense," I say as laughter erupts through the playground, "it was a shit movie. It has literally zero percent on Rotten Tomatoes, which I didn't even know was possible."

"I guess you found other ways to entertain yourself," Madison says coldly.

"Wow, I'm impressed," Everly says. "I didn't know you were such a slut."

I crack my neck, anger pushing up my spine. Okay. So this is how it's going to be. "Madison, truth or dare?" I say.

"Aren't you going to heal Jake?" Kyle cuts in.

"Truth," Madison says, staring at me.

"In middle school, what nickname did you use for Everly behind her back?"

Everly goes still. Chet stops throwing the finger. Kyle and Mark and even Jake all go quiet.

"I don't have to answer that," says Madison. "Mark, truth or—"

"Wait a damn second," says Chet. "No fair. I want to hear this."

"Same," says Everly, crossing her arms.

"This is *my* game," Madison snaps. "I don't have to—"

"Why won't you tell us?" asks Everly.

"It must be really fucking bad," says Chet. "Tell us, Maddie."

Madison glowers, pink creeping up her cheeks. We stare back, rapt. She breathes out, seems to resign herself. "F.S.," she mutters.

"What did it stand for?" I push.

She levels her gaze on me, not Everly, when she answers.

"Fugly Slut."

"What?" says Everly.

Madison has the decency to look apologetic. "Look, I love you, but you were super desperate for attention back then. Around boys, you were just—a lot. So that's what we called you, when you weren't around."

"What the hell?" Everly's voice rises in pitch. "That is so fucked-up. I'm *gay*."

"Yeah, but we didn't—"

"Oh, okay, so is this because you were jealous? Because—oh my God." Everly's eyes narrow into slits. "Is this about me going out with Mark? Still? Because let me just say, you have punished me *enough* for that."

Chet lets out a gleeful whoop. Mark grins a little, cool as ever.

"*No!*" Madison lies, alarmed. Her eyes shoot over to Mark. "No, it—"

"Did you forget freshman year happened? I said I'm sorry. I learned my lesson. And for the record, I asked you if it was okay," Everly says, voice rising higher and higher. "I asked you, and you said it was fine, you said—"

"It's not because of Mark!" Madison insists. "And obviously I don't call you that anymore. Would you get over yourself? It wasn't even because of anything you did, it was more just because I—because I hated you."

Mark and Chet exchange *oh shit* faces.

Everly's jaw drops. "You *hated* me?" she whispers.

"I thought you were annoying," Madison says. "We just—we spent too much time together. But I don't feel that way anymore."

"Yeah, I'd freaking hope so," she snarls. "God! This is—wow. Okay. Wow."

Madison glares at the ground. She pulls at the grass, shredding it into pieces. And somehow, seeing her like that, her eyebrows drawn and her mouth twisted up, the violence begging to burst out of her body—I know, suddenly, that I was delusional, thinking we could ever be friends again. Honestly, I never should have been friends with her in the first place. I've been romanticizing the memories, reliving the good parts to justify coming to the party, but this is who she is. Cruel. Controlling. A gossiper, a liar, and— Anger slams into me like an eighteen-wheeler. And a *thief.* She used my drawings, my designs, to create Ametrine. She stole it from me, and then used it to ostracize me for three whole years. This isn't a reunion gift. This is a middle finger.

Chet returns to throwing Jake's severed finger in the air. Blood whizzes off it in spirals, rains over the hungry grass. "Jake," he says. "I've got another dare for you."

When will it be Chet's turn? Everyone is too scared to target him, and he's only getting worse as the night goes on.

Chet points to the sandbox a few feet away. "I've heard some of the kids from this playground got buried here," he says. At his words, the sand starts to tremble and shift. "You should get in there. Spend some time with them."

The last of the color drains from Jake's face. He clutches at his bleeding hand, wrapped in the scarf Kyle gave him.

"There's plenty of room," Chet says, nodding to Madison.

She taps her watch and the sandbox roils, the earth beneath it opening. We gather around the hole, shoulder-to-shoulder. High, childlike screams well up from the blackness below.

"Climb in, and we'll bury you with them," Chet says.

"Don't worry," Madison adds, "you won't suffocate. You'll just *feel* like you're suffocating."

"How long would I have to stay in?" Jake whispers.

I can't believe he's considering this.

"As long as we want," Chet says. "Go on. Get in. If you

don't"—he smacks Jake's back, as if delivering a joke—"I'll make your real life hell."

Everly tugs at Chet's elbow. "Careful. Remember what happened to Amelia."

"Don't fucking talk about that bitch," Madison snaps.

"Amelia?" I break in. The name triggers a memory: I think she was a girl in my PE class sophomore year. Enormous round glasses, a face that blended into the background. She moved schools two Octobers ago. "What happened to Amelia?" I glance from person to person, but no one answers. "What did you do to her?"

"She was weak," says Madison. Her nostrils flare. "She couldn't handle Ametrine, so she left."

I scan through my memories, trying to get a foothold. Amelia didn't come back to school after the party. She dropped out of Lincoln and stopped posting on social media. Why didn't I check in on her? We weren't close, but I could have said something. Whatever happened in the simulation that year, it broke her. It humiliated her to the point where she couldn't face seeing her classmates again.

How many other kids has Madison been torturing?

Tears gather in the corner of Jake's eyes. He wipes at his nose, blinks fast, his chin wobbling uncontrollably. "I . . ."

"Do it," Madison says. She steps forward and shoves him. He falls to his knees next to the sandbox, cringing away from it. "Don't be a coward."

She winds up to push him again, and I jerk forward, blocking her. For a second we both stand still. She sizes me up, her cheeks twitching with fury.

"I can't believe I ever thought this was a good idea," I say finally. "Nothing has changed. You're just as shitty as I remember."

Her chest rises and falls. A strange blankness spreads across her face.

I bend down and help Jake to his feet. "Come on," I say. "We're leaving."

CHAPTER 13

I TEAR OFF MY HEADSET.

A gasp rips free. Air rushes into my mouth, my *real* mouth, and I lurch forward, my hands colliding with the glass console. Whoa. My vision lags several beats behind the rest of me. I steady myself against the glass, the goggles hanging around my neck.

In the console next to me, Devin is dancing—doing, of all things, the Macarena. It fills me with such a rush of joy, of relief, that I can't wait any longer. I need to get him out of there, away from Madison. I reach for the door.

A lock slides into place. I yank on the handle, try to shake it loose, and a voice sounds overhead. *Please return to the simulation. Your experience is still in process.*

Wait. What?

Please return to the simulation, the voice repeats. *Your experience is still in process.*

No. No. No no no no—

I pull at my haptic suit, noticing suddenly that I still feel the wind from the schoolyard, still feel the crackle of grass under my feet. The suit is live—it's sending sensations to me as if I'm still there. I scrabble at the fastenings, but the suit is secured tightly in the back and I can't reach it, I can't get it off.

Where are the others? Was Vanessa able to get out? I squint around and track down her console. Her door is open, the console empty. Mine is the only one that's locked.

I bang on the glass door, trying to get Devin's attention. I slam my fists until my bones ache. I yell until my voice gives out. Then I sink to the ground and rock back and forth, horror setting in like a fever. There's no getting out of here. I'm trapped—made into one of Madison's playthings.

I rake my hands over my face, panic pulsing through me. It was a setup. Everything, all of this. The invitation to the party. The pretense that she wanted to be friends again. It was all designed to lure me into a final game, a final punishment.

A sob chokes out of my mouth. Tears scorch the corners of my eyes. God. I'm such an idiot. How did I fall for this? Of course Madison doesn't want me back. But still I came running the second she asked me to.

The suit is too tight, the suction cups pinching into my skin. It's screwing with my senses. I try again to pull it off, slit my fingers under my sleeves and yank at the fastenings, but it's no use. A wave of dizziness crashes over me and for a moment it feels like I'm falling—nausea sloshes up and I convulse, gagging, but nothing comes out.

I count my breaths until the vertigo passes. My breath clouds against the wall. Fingers trembling, I write *help* on the glass.

Then I force myself to think. Slowly, I pull the goggles off my neck. I weigh them in my hands.

Madison controls everything in Ametrine. But she made Ametrine from *my* sketches. I know this world as well as she does.

Shaking, I raise the goggles in front of my face. A spark of anger slices through the fear. My grief hardens into something different. Something dangerous.

She wants to lock me in? Fine.

But I won't stay trapped in this console all night. If she wants a game, then I'll play to win.

I breathe in, gritting my teeth. The only way out . . . is to go back in.

CHAPTER 14

I PUT ON THE GOGGLES, AND—

Disappear. Again.

It's like the feeling right before you fall asleep, when you're hurtling through empty space, never landing. My vision squeezes into a pinprick. Colors shriek around me, taunting, swirling. Then the pixels shatter into place and my feet slam into a slick plastic surface. I stagger forward, barely managing to keep my balance.

Voices tangle around me, harsh laughter spraying through the air. This isn't the playground—I've been teleported somewhere new. I reorient, blinking fast. My surroundings smear like watercolors. Where am I?

"I guess I should've mentioned," Madison says, and I whip around in the direction of her voice. "As my special guest, your console works a little differently. We wouldn't want you sneaking off, would we?"

My vision sharpens. There she is—lounging on the ground, her silver hair floating in luscious waves over her head. She holds a Rubik's Cube in one hand. My eyes trace from the toy down to the floor, which is dark blue, gridded like tiles. The floor stretches out about ten feet on all sides. At the end of those ten feet, it cuts off, giving way to darkness.

We're floating in a void, on a giant Rubik's Cube.

Madison fiddles with the one she's holding, and the ground shudders. My throat goes dry. Because of course. She controls the whole thing.

I register Chet next: He stands next to her with his arms crossed, like a bodyguard. The rest of Madison's crew reclines nearby, as if gathered for a picnic. Jake meets my gaze for a moment, then looks away. He clutches at his injured hand, still wrapped in a bloody cloth.

"You know," I say, forcing my voice steady, "I'm wondering if Ametrine is really all it's cracked up to be. If it's so great, you shouldn't have to force people to stay."

"I'm not forcing anyone," says Madison. A cold smile flicks up her mouth. "If you want to go, you can go. I just can't promise you'll enjoy your time in the console."

Because I'd still feel everything. I'd still be trapped, blind, as she controlled all of my pain receptors. My hands clench.

Madison lazily lifts the Rubik's Cube, examining it. "Trust me, bestie. You'll have more fun in here."

Kyle suddenly lunges forward, gripping the ground. Everly seizes Mark's hand. What are they—

Madison laughs, syrup sweet, and then she twists the Rubik's Cube.

The ground soars out from under me. Screams erupt as we're swept onto various sides of the cube. Gravity bends over us, keeping our feet latched to the floor even as it swings us upside down. I hang suspended over endless darkness.

Oh, God. I'm going to throw up. My stomach convulses, nausea sluicing up my throat. For a moment I remember my body in the real world, which only makes it worse. *This isn't real.* My eyes burn in and out of focus. The mouth guard tastes stale between my teeth. The void howls around me, sucking at my skin, hungry. *This isn't real. This isn't real. This isn't—*

Madison's laughter rings out from every direction. It's a physical thing, worming into my eardrums. I can't think straight. I can't remember where I am, if I'm awake or dreaming. Mark darts past me, crawling upside down like a spider. Madison twists the cube again, and we swing back to where we started. I gag, covering my mouth with my hand. My vision spins even as the ground stabilizes.

Clutching my stomach, I squint around, trying to get my bearings. Everly sits with her legs crossed, looking vaguely irritated. Jake doubles over, sheltering his wounded hand. Mark lifts himself over the side of the cube and somersaults over to us. Kyle lies face down, shaking.

Why do they put up with this?

Chet strolls over to Kyle and kicks him in the ribs. "Pissed your pants again?" he said.

Everly cracks a smile. Kyle stirs, groaning.

"Poor Kyle," said Madison, making a pouty face. "You're not so brave offstage, are you?"

Chet clocks my confused expression. "He was our special guest last year," he said. "That little bitch got so scared he pissed his pants in the console. It was hilarious. We got it on video and everything. Now we own his ass."

My eyebrows furrow. Why would Madison target Kyle, of all people? Harmless, anxious Kyle? His only claim to fame was performing in *Cabaret* his freshman year. And yeah, people talked about that performance for weeks. During attendance, teachers paused at his name to compliment him. Scholarship rumors flooded the halls. But it never got to his head. He never acted like a big shot because of it.

My muscles tighten when I realize. Madison was in that play too. She had maybe two lines in the whole thing. And Madison could never stand being upstaged.

So she lured him to Ametrine. Humiliated him. Got it all on video. No wonder he didn't audition for the musical this year. I'm certain Madison did.

Dread creeps up my spine. Kyle is nobody to her—just some kid who stole a bit of attention. Madison and I have bone-deep history. We've hurt each other in ways only best friends can. If that's how she treated Kyle, then what is in store for *me*?

As if in response, Madison rises to her feet. She tucks her Rubik's Cube into her jumpsuit pocket, flicks her wrist, and a fizzy orange drink appears in her hand. She slinks toward me, eyes glittering.

I take a step back. Her smile widens.

"So," she says, holding out the drink to me. "I'm just as shitty as you remember?"

I don't know why I take the drink. Some ridiculous impulse toward politeness, maybe, or an attempt to hide how scared I am. But I don't sip it. The glass sweats, cold against my fingers. All of Madison's friends watch, tracking my reaction.

Madison leans in, her lips brushing against my ear. "I think your memory could use a little refresh. How about we play another game, just the two of us?"

Before I can respond she taps her watch, and everything goes black.

We surge through empty space, wind screaming in our ears. The simulation coils, contracts, then bursts back into clarity.

We respawn in the basement of my old house. Each detail is perfectly rendered: my collages hanging all over the walls, the lumpy red couch, the clunky desktop computer. My chest twinges when I see the bookcase with all my dad's World War I history books. This was our favorite spot to hang out during middle school. Safe from adult eyes, my friends and I spent hours playing Truth or Dare, Kiss Marry Kill, Spin the Bottle—anything that gave us an excuse to tell secrets and touch each other.

Madison shoves me, pointing toward the closet. We played Seven Minutes in Heaven there once. Everyone screeched when Madison spun the bottle and it landed on me (*two girls?! What!*) and in the closet we sat across from each other as our friends jeered outside the door.

I remember that day so clearly. Madison had leaned against the wall, rolled her eyes, and said about our friends outside, "They're the dumbest people alive." Then she adjusted her jean jacket and took out a tube of lip gloss. She examined it, as if checking its surface for dirt. "But we should do it, anyway. Right? For practice."

My mouth went dry. I shoved a strand of hair behind my ear and tried very, very hard to not to panic. "For practice," I had agreed.

She applied the lip gloss, smiled, and leaned forward. The smell of cherries drifted over my face. Our lips touched for less than two seconds. Then we jerked apart, laughing, amazed with ourselves.

When we went back outside, we told everyone that nothing had happened.

Now Madison shoves me again, and I stagger toward the door. My hands close over the handle. But when I open it, the door doesn't lead to the closet. It leads to Madison's childhood bedroom.

I step inside, Madison right behind me. It smells exactly how I remember it, like a Japanese Cherry Blossom wallflower plug from Bath and Body Works. The synthetic scent stings my nose. Languid purple light leaks out from a lava lamp by her bed. A half-finished graphic novel lies open on her desk.

All these things must be lost in the real world to Goodwill and trash cans. Seeing them here, my fingers twitch with the urge to collage. I want to tear out a page from her graphic novel, steal one of the photos hanging over her desk. I want to collect as much proof as possible, sort through all her objects to see which ones still have memories trapped inside, and then remake all of it into a new story. But the materials are trapped here. I can't bring anything back to the real world.

Movement flickers over the dresser mirror and I turn to look at myself.

But the face in the mirror isn't mine. I've been transformed into middle school Madison—no more than thirteen years old.

CHAPTER 15

IT'S STRANGE, SEEING HER FACE AGAIN. IT'S EVEN weirder being the one wearing her skin. I touch my cheek and middle school Madison's hand mimics the movement. Her cheeks are rounder than I remember, her fingers riddled with hangnails. A flush of acne speckles her chin. Exhaustion darkens her eyes. But everything else matches my memory. This is the Madison I knew. A confusing affection rushes into my chest.

"You think you know better than me?" Madison says.

I turn in the direction of her voice, but Madison has disappeared. I'm alone in her childhood bedroom. Goose bumps prickle down my arms. I can feel her watching me from wherever she is.

"If you're so smart," her voice says, "then let's see if you can make it through the worst night of my life."

I meet my eyes again in the mirror. Middle school Madison stares back, an expression of confusion on her face. She is—I am?—wearing a greasy pair of sweatpants and a yellow hoodie. I remember this outfit from our old sleepovers. Back when

Madison Pembroke wasn't *Madison Pembroke,* but just another kid, awkward and insecure like the rest of us.

My eyes catch on the bulletin board over her desk. Cheesy digital photos hang over the frame, almost all of them featuring the two of us. Madison and I grinning outside her parents' house, midway through a picnic in the driveway. A selfie outside the local movie theater. Countless reminders of countless days together. I recognize some of the photos from the collage I made for her. Seeing them makes my throat tighten.

Madison's voice rings out again, as if from an intercom in the ceiling. "Get a move on! You don't want to be late for the eighth-grade dance, do you? Your *best friend* is picking you up soon."

I stand frozen, confused. Before I can figure out what to do, pain explodes up my back.

I lurch forward, seizing the desk for balance. A choking sound rips out my mouth as pain screeches up my spine, burning and digging into my muscles. It feels like someone electrified me with a cattle prod.

Madison's laugh circles overhead.

I grind my teeth, bracing myself against the pain. "What the hell is this?"

She keeps laughing, unseen.

"Madison, *what is this*? What are you—"

Another crack of pain slices up my spine, snatching the

words from my mouth. I cringe against the attack, gasping. When it passes, I don't give myself time to think. I make a break for the door.

I cross the space in seconds. My fingers close around the handle and scalding heat bursts into my hands, sending me cringing back into the room. The door is rigged, hot enough to break skin. Blisters bubble up on my palms, aching.

"Wrong move," Madison's voice says. "You can't go to the dance without getting dressed up first, can you?"

A blister pops, spewing yellow pus. I groan in pain, hobbling back toward her dresser. But I still don't get it. What am I supposed to—

A new wave of pain jolts through me, this time hitting me in the ribs. I double over, yelling out.

"You're not going to change? Or do your hair?" Madison taunts.

Breath hisses between my teeth. Hatred crowds my thoughts, my fingers itching to punch something. But as I stand there, bent over and clutching my stomach, finally her instructions register. I think that I understand her game. For whatever reason, Madison wants me to go through the night of the eighth-grade dance, as the past version of herself. Each "wrong" move results in a penalty . . . a penalty that's so painful it's hard to think straight.

Hands shaking, I slide open Madison's top dresser drawer. A silky red dress gazes up at me. I pick it up and unfold it, letting the curves of the fabric fall to full length. The overhead light catches on the fabric's glossy texture. It casts the dress into shifting, mesmerizing shades of flame. This seems like the right move. Good enough to wear to a school dance. I start to pull off my sweatshirt.

An electric shock blasts into me. I flinch back, cursing.

"Bree says that dress makes you look too bony," says Madison. "Like an angsty little skeleton. You're supposed to look *pretty* tonight."

What? That doesn't—did I say that to her? I mean, maybe I did. I was always comparing my body to hers back then. That's middle school. But it doesn't matter. I don't have time to protest, and I don't want to give her any excuse to attack me again. I shove the dress back in the drawer and rummage through the other options. A slinky pink dress, a yellow romper, and—there. The icy-blue one, from our old pictures. This is the one. I remember it.

I tug off my sweatpants and slide the dress over my head. Then I wait, tense, for confirmation.

Nothing happens. No pain, no attack.

I breathe out slowly, every muscle bunched up. I got it right this time. Thank God.

I move on to the makeup. An enormous white bag bulges next to the dresser mirror, crammed with beauty products. The outside of the bag reads, in girly script, HELLO BEAUTIFUL.

I unzip the bag and sort through Madison's makeup. Pain

radiates out from the blisters on my hands. Yellow pus drips down my fingers.

She could open a beauty store with the amount of makeup in this bag. Four tubes of mascara, dark and light bronzers, two eyelash curlers, a glittery box of eyeshadow, both liquid and pencil eyeliners—and everything in at least three different colors. Even before her parents were billionaires, Madison lived like a princess.

I roll a tube of purple eyeliner in my hand, tempted. It would be hilarious to see middle school Madison wearing edgy makeup. Why did she even have this? She hated bold colors, said they made you look like a slut.

A baseball bat slams into the side of my face. Hot agony rips into my cheekbone, reverberating through my skull. My vision goes black, and I wake up on the ground, the eyeliner fallen from my hand. It wasn't a baseball bat; it was another invisible attack from Madison. A punishment for considering the wrong type of makeup.

"You want to have a *classy* look, idiot," Madison's voice says overhead. "Bree got you that purple eyeliner as a joke, because she knew you'd look terrible in it."

I rub my temples, a tremble whimpering up my shoulders. The story registers, but I remember it being more lighthearted, a loving gag gift. I wanted to make her laugh. Madison makes it seem like I was trying to insult her.

I clamber to my feet, turning back to the dresser. A deep, throbbing headache presses into the backs of my eyes. If I want to survive this, I need to do what Madison wants, the way she wants it. That means getting into her middle school mindset. Remembering what she looked like that night at the dance, what she *wanted* to look like. I close my eyes for half a heartbeat, trying to visualize it. But I need to move fast. No more lingering, no reminiscing.

My hands plunge back into the makeup bag and then I'm carving middle school Madison's face into something sharp. Cold silver eyeshadow. A streak of bronzer that reveals, suddenly, her cheekbones. Thin bladed eyeliner hooking past the corners of her eyes. I work fast, instinctively, and this time, the real Madison doesn't interrupt me.

As a final touch, I dab some cherry lip gloss onto my mouth. I stand back from the mirror, studying Madison's—my—reflection. A pang of insecurity twists up my stomach. She still looks a little awkward. This version of Madison is thirteen, after all. But her skin seems smooth, her cheeks warm and pink, and the dress is gorgeous. Her hair looks fine the way it is, wavy and reaching down to her shoulders. She's ready.

As if granting approval, the bedroom door creaks open. I sprint toward it, slipping between the boiling frame, and run headfirst into—

Me.

I mean, middle school me. Bree from the night of the eighth-grade dance. I hit her head-on, shoulders clashing, nearly knocking her down.

"Shit, sorry," I say automatically.

She jerks back, eyes flashing. "Walk much?"

Her natural brown hair shimmers. New combat boots gleam off her feet. She wears a green dress, the color so bright it absorbs all the light in the room.

For a long moment, I stare at her. A mixture of emotion tangles somewhere beneath my collarbone. The Bree standing in front of me is only vaguely recognizable. This was me before my dad got arrested, before I lost everything. Her eyes glint, bored and arrogant. She smacks a mouthful of mint gum. I want to touch her shoulder, draw her into a hug, but at the same time I kind of want to slap her.

Is this what I actually looked like? This version of me seems too cold, too put together to be accurate. But so far, all the details in Ametrine have been perfectly replicated. Down to every birthmark, every ridge in the floor. How much has Madison exaggerated, and how much is true to her memory? She's obviously biased against me. Still, a seed of truth lives under every lie.

The past version of Bree looks me—middle school Madison—up and down. "I thought you said you were ready."

I open my mouth, but no words come out. A creepy prickling feeling coats my tongue.

"I *am* ready," I say, in middle school Madison's voice. It comes out like a question.

Bree's eyebrows shoot up. "You're not going to do your hair?"

I touch my hair. "I . . ."

An electric shock stabs into my hip. Madison's voice hisses overhead, "Don't just stand there! Explain yourself."

I wind a strand of hair between my fingers. Anxiety tightens my stomach. "I thought it looked good like this."

Bree lets out a huff of laughter. "Yikes. Well, come on. Don't worry about it, I'll do it for you in the car."

I follow her down the hall and into the kitchen. Grandma Edie hovers by the door, her white hair piled into a bun on the top of her head. Her mouth opens in delight at the sight of us.

"You two look like angels," she says. "Come and give me a hug before you go."

Grandma Edie, alive again. Standing right there in front of us, in Madison's old kitchen. Love blooms through my chest. She's wrapped in a light blue bathrobe, eyes soft and sleepy. She reaches her arms out, beckoning.

I move toward her, and my legs seize with agony. The muscles cramp and spasm, and I stumble a step back from her.

"Don't even think about it," Madison's voice says. "Bree thinks Grandma Edie is embarrassing."

"That is not true," I spit out, and another wave splinters up my legs. I consider pushing against it on principle, hugging this avatar of Grandma Edie even if it makes me pass out. But the pain is too much. I need to keep going.

I limp after Bree, leaving Grandma Edie crestfallen in the kitchen. *She's not real,* I remind myself, a jagged sadness knifing between my ribs. *Grandma Edie is dead. It isn't her.* But still, I want to go back. I want to hug her again.

We step out into the navy-blue night. Nervous stars push through the clouds. Dampness clings to the breeze, creating a filmy texture that itches in my throat. My mom's old Cadillac hums in the driveway, waiting for us.

Bree opens the car door. She instructs me—middle school Madison—to sit on the floor in front of her so she can "fix my hair." My mom, three years and an entire lifetime younger, greets middle school Madison with bright enthusiasm. She compliments my dress and *wows* at the silvery makeup.

Bree rolls her eyes. "Can you not talk to us? We just wanted a ride," she says.

Bree twists at my hair, pulling it into a tight braid. Every time I wince, or try to adjust my seating position, the real Madison hits me with a punishing shock.

"Stay still. Don't you want to look pretty?" the real Madison says. "Let your *friend* work her magic."

The car jerks over a pothole, and Bree wrenches at the braid. I force myself to stay still, biting down on the inside of my cheek. I don't care what Madison says. There's no way I was this much of a dick in middle school. It's exaggerated, a caricature of the real thing. It must be.

My mom drives us out of Madison's gated neighborhood. The air-conditioning crackles through the air vents, dry and smelling of leather. My mom tosses back well-meaning questions every few minutes, and Bree shuts her down each time, groaning about how annoying she is.

Bree ties off the braid. "Way better," she says. "Now it's not as embarrassing to be seen with you."

Her tone is light, playful. But the comment lands like a punch to the throat. I hoist myself onto the seat and buckle up.

"So." She lowers her voice, leans in closer. "Is tonight the night?"

The newly done braid hangs over my shoulder, identical to the pictures. Trying to avoid another punishment, I play along. "The night for what?"

"The night you're finally making your move on Mark," says Bree.

A weird, guilty feeling stirs in me.

"Say yes," the real Madison instructs me, her voice floating through the car. "You know it's true."

"Yep," I say, in middle school Madison's voice. "Tonight's the night."

"Are you excited?" Bree asks.

"So excited," I answer.

Red streetlights dance across the windows. A light rain

starts to patter into the glass, melting the colors together. Mom scrolls through the radio, pausing at a bubblegum pop song. *I got my best friend back,* the singer croons. *He was no good for you.*

"You've totally got this," Bree says. "He'll be all over you. Guaranteed. Boys like it when you put in a little effort. He'll appreciate how hard you worked to look good tonight."

The comment stings, sharp and quiet. I shrink in my seat and look out the window.

Bree's mom pulls into the Lincoln Academy parking lot. The door to the gym is propped open, music streaming out into the street. She turns around with a stern expression and lectures us about making good decisions, then we're ducking through the rain, giving our names to the teacher volunteering at the entrance.

Inside, string lights throw a romantic hue onto the walls. Upbeat music blares through the speakers. Teachers prowl the perimeter as middle schoolers mill around in ugly suits and dresses.

The déjà vu nearly bowls me over. This is so ridiculously specific, like when you're at the grocery store and randomly catch a scent you recognize from childhood. It's deeper than nostalgia, closer to time travel.

Under different circumstances, it could be delightful. Browsing through memories, reliving favorite moments. I could make a thousand collages from the colors in this one room. But that's not why I'm here.

"Oh my God," says Bree, only loud enough for me to hear. "Check out Everly. That's *so* funny. She looks like a total pick-me girl."

Across the gym, Everly grooves on the dance floor, her yellow dress swishing. A giant smile lights up her face when she spots us. She waves and motions us over.

I start toward her, and a shock rams through my temple. My head feels like it's about to split open.

"You heard Bree," says Madison's voice. "Everly looks like a pick-me girl. You can't associate with that."

My jaw aches with tension. I scan the room, trying to figure out what I'm supposed to do. Bree prances off into the crowd, chatting with the other classmates.

The goal of the game, it seems, is to avoid embarrassment. In that case it's safest to hang back and wait the night out somewhere quiet. I retreat to the back of the gym and lean against the wall, preparing to settle in, but before I can relax Madison zaps me in the stomach.

"Don't be antisocial," her voice says as I double over. "Everyone is looking at you. They'll notice that you're standing alone back here like a creepy loser."

Vision swimming, I force myself to reassess. A strand of hair jumps free, falling into my eyes, and I shove it behind my ear. A crowd of students hovers at the snack table, talking and cracking each other up. Getting a snack seems reasonable. Normal. At the very least, it will give my hands something to do.

I hobble over, pain lighting up my legs. The sticky gym floor clings to my shoes, each step making a popping sound. When I arrive, I offer the group of students a bland smile. Their eyes move past me and they keep talking—except for one girl. She stares at me through thick-rimmed glasses, her mouth set in a straight line. A weight drops through me as I look back. As I recognize her.

It's Amelia. The girl who changed schools after being tortured in Ametrine.

But this isn't the eighth-grade version of her. This Amelia is tall enough to be a sophomore at least. The baby fat has eroded from her cheeks.

Horror crawls down my throat. I try to speak, but no words come out. As Amelia studies me, unsmiling, blood drips down from behind one of her lenses. It races down her cheek like a tear.

I blink, and she's gone.

What the fuck?

I don't have time to process. I have to stay focused, move fast. I came over here to seem normal, to have a snack. So I force myself to reach for some of the chips. Before I even touch them, a stab of electricity slices up my hand.

"You want sour cream and onion breath?" Madison demands. "Don't be disgusting."

Frustration tears at me. What the hell am I supposed to do then?

Cradling my hand, I limp away from the snack table. A gaggle of classmates are gathered near the dance floor—maybe that's where I'm supposed to be? Grimacing, I join them and attempt some of the half dancing, half swaying they're doing. But of course it doesn't work. Seconds later I'm on the ground again, shocked so hard that something wet floods out my nose. When I touch my face, my hand comes back red. No one notices. I'm alone in a crowd of students, bruises welting across my skin, blood staining my dress, and up ahead on the dance floor I spot Bree, dancing alongside Everly even though she was talking shit about her only minutes ago.

Tears burn in my eyes. I scrub at them, a smear of mascara transferring to my hand, and the absurd thought that rushes in is: *I need to get my shit together. What will Bree think?*

That's when it hits me. Every attack from Madison, all these moments of angst and insecurity, came from middle school Madison trying to impress middle school Bree. The object of this twisted game isn't to avoid humiliation. The goal is to show me what it was like, being my own perfect sidekick. Winning is impossible.

"You can still save the night from total disaster," Madison's voice says into my ear. "Look over there."

An invisible force turns my head, spinning me toward another gaggle of students. Up ahead, I spot an eighth-grade version of Mark Sato.

He looks way more awkward than I remember. Half-grown

facial hair dots his cheeks. His pants are an inch too short, showing a line of white socks. He stands with a group of friends, all of them swaying to the music.

I lick my lips, tasting pennies. My new mission clarifies: get to him, and tell him how I—how middle school Madison feels.

But right as I start to move, the crowd ripples. Someone parts the sea of people, heading straight toward him. I freeze, stomach sinking. Suddenly, I know what's about to happen. The realization crystallizes, sharp as diamond.

Middle school Bree breaks through the crowd and strides toward Mark with a sense of purpose.

I can feel Madison watching me, taking in my reaction. It feels like my whole body is a scab, slicing open under her thumbnail. I never realized that she saw me approach Mark that night. All these years, I thought that I'd gotten away with it.

I hate thinking about this, remembering it, because it's shitty and embarrassing and not who I am anymore. But I don't get a choice right now. This is what happened.

The night of the dance, Madison spent the whole time obsessing over Mark. Actually, she had spent the last *year* obsessing over him, but the night of the dance was the worst. She wouldn't talk about anything else. She wouldn't eat, wouldn't dance, wouldn't do anything but stand somewhere near him and mess with her hair. It was a buzzkill. But worse, it made me feel unwanted. Like having me with her wasn't enough. She was so ridiculously beautiful, so lethally intelligent, so funny and weird and terrifying, and all she wanted to do was stare at some idiot guy while I was right there next to her.

I didn't have words for this feeling yet, but if she tried to kiss me that night—for real, not just for practice—I would have let her. If she said she wanted to run away, I would have booked the bus ticket. I would have done anything, anything in the world, to move her gaze from him to me.

Instead, she kept hovering near Mark and I waited by her side, sipping lukewarm fruit punch and feeling sorry for myself.

She only moved from her stakeout once, to go to the bathroom. And during that time, I . . . I guess I wanted to see what was so special about him.

Or maybe I wanted to end her obsession. Maybe I wanted to ruin any chance she had with him, once and for all, because I was jealous.

Either way, it was only one dance. I didn't think Madison was looking. I didn't think she'd see.

But now, standing in middle school Madison's shoes, I realize I was wrong.

Middle school Bree taps Mark's shoulder. He turns around and greets her, a wide grin splitting his face. She gestures toward the dance floor, and he nods.

Blood trickles down my lip, cuts a tangy flavor into my mouth. The dim room seems grimy all of a sudden, as haunted as a crime scene. Watching them talk, I feel dirty and humiliated.

Mark's friends hoot as he and Bree wander to the dance floor. Bree plays with her dress, swishing it around her knees. Mark jokingly straightens his tie. Then they wrap their arms around each other.

"You're just going to watch her do this?" Madison's voice says, yanking me back into the game. A rip of electricity shatters through my spine. "Try again. Stop her!"

My lungs constrict, seem to spasm. I cough hard, splattering blood into my elbow. The scene resets, bringing us back to the moment when Bree walks up to Mark.

The song that was playing starts over again. Bree breaks through the crowd. I stumble forward, trying to beat her to him. But my legs seize right as I approach his friend group, and I'm thrown backward by another *zap*. I land hard on my back, my head cracking into the gymnasium floor.

White-hot agony flushes through my skull. My hand scrabbles against my chest, feeling for a heartbeat. I need to remember where my real body is, feel my actual blood thrumming beneath the haptic suit, because this is getting too fucking real. Pain twitches through my rib cage and I breathe in fast, hard gulps.

Suddenly, I wonder: can you *die* in Ametrine? I think these electric shocks could injure my real body. I think they could stop my heart.

The scene resets again. And again. And again. Every time, I try to get to Mark before Bree does. I try to stop her. And every time, I'm thrown back by a scream of electricity. Strength saps from my limbs. Blood runs out my nose, my mouth, the corners of my eyes. Finally, I give up, curling on the ground as the scene resets again. Shock after shock punishes me. Broken sobs shake my chest.

Madison says, "I wanted to die that night. Do you know what that feels like?"

She hits me with a crushing, million-volt zap. It roars through my entire body, drilling into my bones, the marrow, every blood vessel exploding at once. A scream latches in my mouth, never leaving.

Everything goes dark as she finally, mercifully kills me.

CHAPTER 16

EXCEPT I'M NOT DEAD. NOT YET.

I don't want to open my eyes. The gym floor sticks to my cheek. My head is too heavy to lift.

I hear a popping sound and crack an eye open. Present-day Madison stands above me, watching. A muscle in her jaw jumps. She doesn't crouch down, doesn't bring herself to my level.

"You knew how much I liked him," she says, voice low.

Hot, shaking rage coils in my belly. I push myself off the ground with quivering arms.

"You pounced on him that night, just because you could," Madison says. A deadly brightness shines in her eyes. "Just to *humiliate* me."

"Are you kidding me?" I whisper. My voice is hoarse with fury. I step forward and try again, throwing all my breath behind the words. "Are you KIDDING me? This—*this*—is what you've been holding on to for all these years? One night where I made a stupid mistake? I was *thirteen*, Madison. This game—this fucking game, you've been *torturing* me all night and you—

you—what the fuck is wrong with you?" Tears scald my cheeks, mix with the blood. My voice cracks. "I thought you wanted to be friends again."

"You sabotaged me," says Madison. Her eyes narrow to slits. "All my life, you made me feel like nothing."

"It wasn't like that," I say. "And besides, that was years ago. Everly dated Mark, and you stayed friends with her. I wasn't trying to—"

"Everly asked my permission," Madison says. "And anyway, I've dealt with her. But you . . . It was always Queen Bree back then. Everything was about you. What *you* thought, what *you* liked, what *you* wanted."

"That's bullshit. Everly dated him for months, but it's okay because she asked permission. I dance with him *one time,* and I get tortured for years?" My voice rises as courage surges through me. "I don't buy it."

"What are you trying to say?"

"This isn't just about Mark. You and Everly were friends. But you and I were—"

My courage flatlines. The words die in my mouth. Because there's no real name for what Madison and I were to each other. We never defined the tension between us. We never acknowledged how viciously we loved each other, or how that love became hopelessly ensnared with resentment. How it all turned into this spiral of obsession that was impossible to crawl out of.

"—we were different," I finish, stupidly.

Something in Madison's expression flickers. "Don't," she says.

"That day in the closet," I say. "Seven Minutes in Heaven."

"Fuck you," she says. "This is so typical. No way could this be about you doing something shitty to me. No, it just *has* to be about how I secretly had a crush on you. Fuck you."

"Madison," I try again, but she speaks over me.

"This isn't about that. You don't get to—to *reduce* this to whatever angsty closeted bullshit that was. Tonight is about how you treated me as your 'friend.' You've somehow convinced yourself that *I'm* the bully. That I'm the only one who did anything wrong." She taps her watch. "You have no idea what I felt like that night."

The middle school versions of Mark and I disappear. In their place, Madison summons a hologram of present-day Devin and herself. They stand with their arms entangled, leaning into one another. The Devin hologram traces the Madison hologram's cheek with his thumb, pushes a thread of her hair behind her ear.

"Stop," I say. My head pounds, louder and louder. My lungs squeeze with panic. But I can't look away. "Madison, stop it."

Devin slides his hand under Madison's jaw and gazes into her eyes with that familiar gentleness. The hologram of Madison giggles. She whispers something in his ear. Then she drags her hand into Devin's hair and pulls him into a kiss.

"Stop!"

They keep making out, in graphic high definition. Devin slips his tongue into Madison's mouth. Madison tugs at his hair, laughs into the kiss. The other students cheer them on.

"Do you get it?" snaps the real Madison. "Do you see?"

I want to shove her to the ground. I want to take this feeling out of my body and slam it into her teeth. "You're fucking sick," I say.

"Say you get it," Madison says. A cold smile lifts her mouth. "Say you understand."

Devin's arm tightens around Madison's waist. He somehow pulls her even closer, his hand drifting to Madison's ass.

I cringe, covering my eyes. "I get it! Okay? I get it. Please, stop."

"But *you* didn't stop. Because nothing is ever enough for Queen Bree."

"What are you talking about? All we did was dance together."

"Not true," Madison spits. "Stop playing dumb. The next day, you told him I was obsessed with him. That I watched his TikTok videos hundreds of times a day. That I kept riding my bike past his house to look into his windows. I rode by *once*. One time! I never should've told you. I opened up to you, I trusted you, and you used it against me."

Guilt flashes through me, cutting through the haze of anger. I do remember kind of . . . exaggerating to Mark. I just—all Madison did was pine over him. It consumed our interactions, ate into all our time together. I guess I thought that if he didn't like her back, then things might go back to normal. That it could just be the two of us again.

Christ. I bury my face in my hands. What was I thinking? She didn't deserve that. No one does.

But then another voice interrupts, from the back of my head: *This happened three years ago*. Before my dad got arrested. Before we lost the house. Everything has changed since then. *I've* changed. What are we doing, arguing about some boy? Like, yeah, maybe I screwed up with Mark. I acted like an idiot. But that was middle school. When shit got real, where was Madison?

"You're the one who ditched me after my dad got arrested," I say. Defensiveness heats my face. "You made me feel like I was some broke loser. Like I wasn't good enough to hang out with you, with any of you. The thing with Mark—that was one mistake. You've made my life hell for years."

Madison stares at me, her mouth slightly open. For a split second, something in her gaze opens, and I realize she's genuinely astonished. "One mistake," she repeats. She shakes her head, pushing her walls back up. "You really don't get it."

"Madison—"

"You don't remember." She scoffs, a biting sound. "Fine. Cute. Let's go through a few examples then, shall we?"

We catapult into a new setting. This time we're in the

school cafeteria, surrounded by friends, and the middle school version of me blabbers about a movie Madison and I watched together.

"When we got to the part where the grandma dies, Madison started *bawling*," past me says. "Like, full on, snot everywhere. It was the most pathetic thing I've ever seen."

"It was a sad movie!" past Madison says. She wears a sparkly shirt with a peace sign on it. An embarrassed flush colors her neck.

"No, it just made you think of your grandma," past me says. Then, to the table, "She's obsessed with her grandma. Like, they kiss each other on the mouth. It's so gross."

"We do not!" Madison's ears turn bright red. The table roars with laughter.

"They totally do. It's disgusting. They basically make out."

The scene changes again. This time we're in Mr. Hemlock's history class, and past Madison sits down next to me. Past me reaches out and touches Madison's hair.

"Your split ends are so stylish," past me says, loud enough for our classmates to hear. "You make it look cool. It's, like, ugly-hot." Then she goes through a whole laundry list of beauty tips while Madison's shoulders curl in further and further.

Then we're in Madison's mansion, hanging out in her dad's bunker. Mr. Pembroke is obsessed with the apocalypse and has always kept this room full of canned food, water jugs, and a whole set of security camera screens, just in case. Madison and

I liked to hang out in there and watch the security footage in real time.

"I feel like you're different around other people," past Madison says. She chews a hangnail on her thumb. "Like you're not my best friend anymore. Or like you're trying to show off by being mean to me."

"That is so not true," past me says. She fiddles with the security camera screen, barely paying attention. "You sound crazy. Why are you always trying to start crap?"

"I'm not starting crap."

"Everything I say to them is true," past me says. "And it's funny, so I'm gonna share it. You're too sensitive."

"I'm just saying—"

"Why do you even care what they think of you? You don't need them. We have each other."

My face actually hurts from cringing. I remember each one of these moments, and it's awful seeing them laid out like this.

Madison's grudge isn't about Mark. It's about how I manipulated her, all the time. These scenes are waking up other memories too, a thousand horrifying examples. Mocking Madison's parents. Spreading rumors about her in the bathroom and insisting Everly was the one to blame.

Finally, the truth clicks into place and shame fills me down to my toes. Our friendship didn't end when my dad got arrested. It had been dying for years, because of the way I treated her.

Madison wasn't the queen bee of middle school.

I was.

My first thought?

Thank God Devin isn't here to see this.

I turn to present-day Madison. Her eyes are fixed on the holograms of us, two kids arguing in a bunker. Her mouth is set in a straight line.

"Madison," I breathe out. The words hurt, they feel like betrayal, but I force them free. "I'm so sorry."

She doesn't respond. Her expression seems frozen in place.

"I was terrible to you," I say. "I think I blocked a lot of this out. It's like—with everything that was happening at home, I think I just . . ." I trail off. Excuses won't help. "I'm sorry."

Madison doesn't move. She glares at the hologram of us, arms crossed, her fingernails digging into her arms. For a second I'm not sure if she's really there, or if the simulation is buffering. But then, finally, she speaks.

"You treated me like I was your little sidekick," she says. "Like I was nothing."

A lump builds in my throat. She's right.

"When I tried to talk to you about it, you said I was crazy," she says. "You never listened. You only cared about yourself."

I swallow hard, force myself to speak. "You didn't deserve that."

I touch her shoulder and she jerks back. But now, finally, she's looking at me.

"I've changed since then," I tell her. "But that doesn't undo what happened, how I treated you. I wish I could go back and fix it. We were just kids. I was insecure, and I was jealous—of Mark, of Everly, of you. I didn't know how to handle it, so I lashed out. But you deserved better. I loved you so much. I'm sorry, Madison."

Her lips part, trembling as she breathes out. She uncrosses her arms, steps closer to me. For a long moment, we gaze at one another. Chills erupt down my arms as she leans in.

"You're sorry?" she whispers.

Our faces are centimeters apart. I can smell her cold breath, her cherry lip gloss.

"I'm sorry," I confirm softly.

Her pupils shrink to pinpricks. Our hands brush. I can sense the younger version of her, straining under the surface. For a second, I think we might hug. That she might wrap me up and welcome me home again.

"Good," she spits.

Then she jabs her watch, and we hurtle into darkness.

CHAPTER 17

WE DROP INTO A BLACK LIGHT RAVE, CRUSHED on all sides by dancers. Music blasts through the room, shaking the floor. Psychedelic color bends off the walls. Glow sticks glitter in people's hair, and everyone's teeth radiate white.

Madison is gone.

Fear crawls down my spine. Where did she go? What is she planning? I don't recognize this place from my sketches.

I need to get out of here, find someplace safe to wait it out. A few feet away, Chet grinds on a blond NPC. Jake chugs a glass of fluorescent purple liquid. No sign of Kyle. But I recognize another girl from my math class, someone who isn't in Madison's inner circle, which means—

"Devin," I whisper. I stand on my tiptoes, scanning the crowd. Sweat itches under my clothes, burrows into my skin. *"Devin?"*

Dubstep pounds through the room like a monstrous heartbeat. The sound swallows everything. But if the other partygoers are here, then Devin should be too. So where is he? Is he okay? I have to talk to him, warn him.

I push through the crowd, the party lights spasming around me. I shout his name, my voice raw with panic, lost under the noise. It's useless. *I'm* useless. The crowd clambers around me, hundreds of strangers singing and laughing, but I'm all alone.

A sob builds in my throat. Devin didn't even want to come to Madison's party. Why didn't I listen? Maybe Madison is right. Maybe I'm the same asshole she knew in middle school. Selfish. Controlling. Pathetic.

My knees buckle. I cover my ears, hands shaking, and I'm about to sink to the floor, about to shut down, give up, when I spot him.

My favorite person.

He dances with his arms over his head. Chin tilted up, like he's drinking the air. His long hair ripples. Sheer relief lights up every one of my nerve endings. God, I want to hug him. I need that warmth, that comfort. I want to feel the weight of his arms, his breath against my neck as he tells me it'll be okay. He's right there. I could get to him, I know I could. But then the crowd tightens—the music cuts off—and all the lights spin to the front of the room. There, in a ring of spotlights, a stage rises out of the ground, carrying Madison Pembroke.

My confidence shrivels, the hope in my chest dying.

On stage, Madison pulls a microphone out of thin air. The crowd screams. She taps the microphone with a playful faux concern, as if testing whether it works, as if *anything* she summoned wouldn't work here. Then, with a flourish, she brings it to her lips and purrs, "Hello, Ametrians."

The crowd goes nuts. Full-on screeching, chanting her name. One NPC hysterically wails, like they've been waiting all their life for this moment.

Madison makes a teasing *Who, me?* expression. Her teeth glare out freakishly bright under the black light. "Oh, stop it," she says. "You all are too much. No, give it up for *yourselves.* What a perfect night, right? This has been an amazing group."

More cheers. I scan the room for an exit, but the crowd locks me in on all sides.

"Let's see the highlights!" Madison says, and taps her watch.

Behind her, a giant projection blazes to life. It rolls through a montage from the night, showing off the fun side of the party—the side I didn't get to see. People cliff jumping, race car driving, climbing the New York City skyline. Dancing, laughing, making out with cute NPCs. In one clip, Devin takes a bite of fancy cheesecake and moans.

"This is our best night in Ametrine yet," Madison continues. "Another year of absolutely crushing it. And it wouldn't be possible without all of you."

The highlight reel keeps playing behind her. Where did all of this footage even come from? She wasn't there for any of it, she was too busy torturing us in other parts of the simulation.

As the images flash through, one after another, it occurs to me that everything in Ametrine must be recorded. Not just one-off humiliations, like what happened to Kyle. Knowing Madison, she has years of footage. She's been gathering data on her classmates and will hold every moment of this night hostage.

"I have one more game for you all tonight," Madison says. "Does anyone have a guess?"

Shouts pour out of the crowd. She giggles, holds her hand to her ear. The shouts escalate, everyone losing their minds.

Madison flicks her wrist, and her closest friends teleport to her side. Kyle, Chet, Everly, and Mark gaze out onto the crowd, hands behind their backs.

"The game is . . ." Madison pauses dramatically. "*Assassins.*"

On cue, her friends pull out weapons. Gleaming silver machetes. Chainsaws. Flame throwers. Everly offers a wicked smile and slings a dagger into the crowd. A junior leaps up and snatches it out of the air.

"Everyone will receive a slip of paper with the name of your target," Madison drawls. "The winner of this game gets my utmost respect . . . *and* a birthday party of their own at my family's mansion."

Shock billows through the room, swelling into hysterical excitement. Her friends keep throwing weapons off the stage and into eager hands.

"Of course, I wouldn't want to play favorites, or for any of my friends to have an unfair advantage," she says, teeth glinting. She raises her wrist up to the crowd, showing off the watch.

"So for the duration of the game, I'll disable my location services. Everyone is now off the grid."

I try to get Devin's attention, but he's looking down, reading a slip of paper. Where did he get that? Looking around, I realize he's not the only one. Along with the weapons they're gripping, slips of paper have materialized into everyone's hands—everyone but me.

I peer over people's shoulders, scanning the papers. Everyone's slip says the same thing, written in Madison's signature handwriting. One name, over and over again.

BREE

"My oldest friend has volunteered to help," Madison says.

The emergency exits in the club swing open. Across the crowd, Devin finally looks up, and our eyes meet. His mouth forms my name.

"She has three lives," Madison says. "Let the hunt begin."

CHAPTER 18

THERE'S NO TIME TO THINK. NO TIME TO wait for Devin. My body takes over, adrenaline splitting through my legs. I sprint toward the exit.

Find me, I think, as I shove aside a cluster of NPCs. Shouts stream out behind me. *Stay alive, Devin, and find me.*

What happens if I die in Ametrine? Kyle pissed himself from fear. Amelia left the school. What if I never come back at all?

I burst out the door, into wild moonlight. The smell of tulips buckles through the air. I know this place. I'm in Madison's garden, surrounded by miles of winding paths through trees, bushes, and flowers. We spent whole weekends here as kids, playing hide-and-seek. Every plant stands straight, pristine. Watching me.

Behind me, the shouts grow louder. The guttural roar of a chainsaw cuts through the air.

If they get to me, I'll feel everything. Every blade, every punch, every rip of skin.

I take off into the garden.

Most of the partygoers are drunk or high by now. It's a

frail advantage, but it's something. They'll be slow, blurry. Within minutes, muscle memory leads me off the path. I dart between rows of sculpted fir trees. Stars fizzle overhead like sparkling water.

I cut through the rosebushes, toward a row of spiral-shaped hedges. Nearby, a voice belts out: "*Over there!*"

If my memory is right—and if this simulation is as detailed as I think it is—

I count the hedges as I run past. One, two—*that one*. I throw a glance over my shoulder, suck in a breath, and lunge into the branches.

Twigs tear at my skin, drawing blood down my arms. But after the initial wall of branches, I burst into a clearing, a space that's about a half-foot long, between the first and second arc of the hedge spiral. Breath splinters in my chest. Sweat coats my arms, my back. Did anyone see me go in?

It doesn't matter—I can't stop now. I count nine steps clockwise around the perfectly pruned spiral, just like I did as a kid. Then I fall to my knees and dig.

Within seconds I find it, nestled in the dirt. My fingers curl around the artifact, the treasure. I pull it free and weigh it in my hands. Madison's old baseball bat. We used to play with this thing for hours, competing over who could hit baseballs the farthest. Grandma Edie outlawed the game after Madison shattered a window. From then on, we played in secret, hiding the bat here.

"Breeeeeezy," Chet's voice sings.

I freeze. He's on the other side of the hedge, mere feet away. Does he know I'm here?

"Come heeeere, Breezy-Breezy-Breezy."

His shadow moves past the branches. Barely breathing, I tighten my grip on the bat.

Other partygoers blunder past, cackling and calling my name. But Chet hangs back, even as they keep going down the path.

"I know you're hiding," he says. "I saw you a minute ago. Scared to show your face, Benson?"

I silently creep closer, clutching the bat like a weapon. His shadow pauses, as if sensing my movement.

"I can't wait to see the look on Madison's face when I kill you," he says.

I raise the bat, hands shaking. Sweat drips down my neck.

"You should just give up," he says. "Turn yourself in, like your pathetic drunk of a dad did to the police."

I burst through the branches, smashing the bat through the air. It cracks into the side of his face with a sickening crunch. His roar of pain follows me up the path as I race back the way I came, leaving the rest of the party to continue searching for me in the garden.

Mulch spits out under my feet as I run. The Pembroke mansion looms ahead. Are there hologram versions of her parents in there, arguing over the dinner table? Is Grandma Edie spooning ice cream in the living room? How far does this world go?

I make it to the sliding glass door that faces the garden. It's unlocked, glides open with a shushing sound. I stumble inside, almost sobbing with relief, and lock the door behind me. Without turning on any of the lights, I burst through the mudroom, round the corner, and find the bathroom. Perfect. I race inside, lock the door, test it, and lock it again. It's good. It's safe. I sink against the wall, clutching the baseball bat to my chest. My heart slams. No windows. No lights. No sound. Nothing to give myself away. I drag my fingers through my hair. A sob breaks out my throat and I cover my mouth with my hand. Finally, sitting there on the cold bathroom tile, I let myself freak out.

I can't make it another four hours. I can't. I need to get out of here. I need help. I need *Devin*. If I can get to him, if he can find me somehow, then I can explain everything. He'll forgive me for being shitty in middle school—that's not the version of me he knows anyway. He'll leave Ametrine if I ask him to. In a heartbeat. I know he would. He never trusted Madison to begin with. He must see how screwed up everything is. If I can find him, we can escape together. We can—

The door rattles. *Fuck*. Who—

"Bree? Are you in there?"

My heart stops. That's Devin's voice. He found me. Somehow, he found me.

The door rattles again. “Bree?”

I fumble with the lock, lightheaded with hope. He’s so close. I can hear him breathing on the other side.

“Are you there, Bree?”

“Shhh, baby,” I whisper. “I’m here. I’m here. Hang on.”

I fling the door open.

But it’s not Devin.

It’s Jake, his mouth stretched into a wide smile.

“Surprise!” he says, a synthetic version of Devin’s voice coming from his mouth.

He tosses a grenade into the bathroom and slams the door shut.

CHAPTER 19

SOUND, FIRST. IT SLASHES PAST MY SKIN, BURROWS into my skeleton, and implodes. I hear my own screams as if from another room. Wails and wails of agony. A wave of blue-white light. Then, silence. The sound stolen from my ears.

The explosion launches me against the bathroom wall, my head cracking against the tile. Shrapnel sticks out of my hands, my chest. Blood, everywhere. My stomach on fire, and I can't breathe, my lungs won't fill, and I'm going to die here, I'm actually going to die.

I tear off my headset, gasping. The console walls swim around me. But the pain doesn't stop. I still can't breathe, my chest aflame, shards of shrapnel lodged in my legs. I pull at my haptic suit, trying to disconnect the suction cups from my skin, at least hold off the pain for a second, but it's no use. My spine snaps and I pitch forward, hitting the glass. Someone is kicking me in the simulation.

I need to go back in. Any time I spend here, my avatar is left vulnerable, slumped on the ground like a sitting duck.

I pull the goggles back on and fall through the dreamlike tunnel.

I respawn on the other side of the mansion, outside again. The pain lifts away. My avatar must have officially "died" in the bathroom with Jake.

The temperature has plummeted. Goose bumps pinch down my arms and my breath hovers in the air. The mansion's long, hooked driveway unfurls ahead of me.

Cold air scratches in my throat. I touch my arms, my stomach, checking that the searing pain is really gone. Relief drips through me. At least for now, I'm okay.

A haunted silence drapes over the estate. Where is everyone? Is it possible I've been given a fresh start? No one else is here, so maybe they don't know where I've respawned—at least, not yet.

Fuck, it's freezing. Mist gathers in the air, dense and smelling sickly sweet. My thoughts scramble out, then reassemble. I need to move, get as far away as possible, before anyone spots me. I have two lives left. What happens when I run out?

I creep down the winding driveway, toward the gate. Maybe if I can escape the Pembroke Estate, I can get back to the world I designed, someplace safer. Maybe no one will even realize I've left, and they'll keep searching the grounds for me until the simulation is over. The driveway looms ahead, endlessly long, the far-off gate wavering like a mirage. I speed up to a jog, gravel spitting out under my shoes. The fog slithers against my face, sticks my hair to my cheeks.

Air whistles past my ear and I flinch to the side, barely

dodging a—what is that? An *arrow*? It slices into the ground inches from me, vibrating with force.

Another arrow shoots past, missing me by about a foot. Someone is coming after me. With a bow.

I break into a sprint down the driveway. The fog tightens around me from all angles so I can't see the gate; I can't tell where I'm running, but I can't stop. I won't. I fling my arms out, reaching blindly, and charge ahead.

An arrow whips past and I yelp, almost lose my footing. Then another shrieks by, and another, and—

A scream shatters out of my mouth. I pitch to the ground, knees striking into pavement, blood spraying out of my arm. An arrow sticks out of my skin, right above the elbow.

I clutch at the injury, wet with blood. My temples squeeze and I blink fast, trying to shake off the dizziness, trying not to scream again.

I want to yank it free, I want it out of me, but pulling it would only cause more blood loss. I have to get up. I have to keep moving. If I stay here, they'll catch me. But oh my God it *hurts*. Mist coats my skin, shimmers like dew. The fog is thinning.

I look over my shoulder. I can see them now. A group of students huddle on the mansion roof, pointing toward me. But they're still far away. I can beat them.

I stumble to my feet and force myself to keep running. With the fog clearing, I can see where I'm going again. The driveway gate shines up ahead, framed on both sides by stone walls. I'm slower now, my balance thrown off and my injured arm wailing, but adrenaline pushes me ahead.

Finally, my hands close around the bars of the gate. I shove, and it clangs, locked. I groan, fighting back a sob. My arm aches in protest. I'll have to climb.

A car engine revs behind me. I turn just in time to see Madison's family Porsche fishtail out, Chet at the wheel.

"No," I hiss, hands tightening around the metal bars. "No, no, *no*—"

I scramble for a hold on the gate, trying to lift myself up. My arm seizes, and the gate is over eight feet tall, but still, I have to make it. There's no other option.

"Feel familiar?" Chet crows out the window. One of his eyes is crusted shut, covered in bruises. "Maybe I should pull a Benson. Get drunk, mangle a leg. Your daddy did it, so it's okay, right?"

Rage boils in my veins. I use it to lift myself halfway up the gate. Sweat slimes between my fingers.

"This is the most pathetic thing I have ever seen," Chet says. "Do you really think you can escape that easily? You really are a dumb fucking bitch."

A crowd of other classmates streams down the driveway, all holding weapons and jeering. Another arrow streaks past and I wrench to the side. My eyes go hot, a sob pushing up behind my sternum. This can't just be a game to them. Their shouts, the twisted glee on their faces, it's impossible to deny.

Everyone here hates me. They are gathering below, looking up at me, and every one of them wants me dead.

I hoist myself farther up the gate, shaking so hard I can barely support my weight. My injured arm rails with agony. Someone throws a knife and I flinch, barely dodging, but I lose my balance.

Someone screams, "*Bitch Benson!*"

A rock smashes into my shoulder, the same side as my arm injury. The pain is too sharp, too sudden, and my grip snaps—for a moment I'm airborne, and as I fall, it feels never ending.

Cheers soar up from the crowd. They quickly clear a space so I land hard on my back, the breath crushed out of me. My vision goes black for half a second, then I return with a start, like waking from a dream. Every part of my body throbs.

Chet backs the car up, blasting the horn triumphantly. The kids part around him, making room. He's angling the car to run me over, make a big, messy scene for everyone to enjoy.

Tears squeeze out the corners of my eyes. God. Maybe I should give up. Let them kill me. At least then everyone would be happy.

Then I see Chet's sick, greedy smile in the windshield. Forget Madison—I never did a damn thing to him. Nothing. And there he is, laughing, making jokes about my father, winding up to kill me. In that moment, I hate him more than anyone. As he smashes the gas pedal, I reach for a stone.

I throw it as hard as I can, straight into the windshield. The glass splinters and Chet swerves, careening off the road. I turn back to the crowd, struggle to my feet, and then—

Pain erupts through my chest. I stagger backward, a hot wetness unspooling from the impact. I look down and find the end of an arrow jutting out of my ribs. A few feet away, Everly stands holding an empty bow.

I don't know why I feel betrayal. Everly was never my friend, always the enemy. I was even worse to her than I was to Madison.

I fall to my knees, choking on blood. Someone hands Everly another arrow, and she loads it onto her bow. The crowd hoots, ecstatic.

But as Everly lets the arrow fly and our eyes connect for an instant, I swear there's something else in her expression—not joy, not hatred. Something closer to pity.

I'm dead before the arrow lands.

The smell of mint leaves, bladed and cool. My nose pressed into dirt, my senses coming back online.

Lying there, I forget for a moment where I am. *Who* I am. Like I could wake up a new person, some innocent partygoer on the winning side. But no. I'm still Bree. Still in Ametrine. I lift my head and see that I'm back in the garden, this time in the herbal section. Rosemary, basil, that sharp-scented mint. I'm about half a mile out from the mansion, another useless head start.

This is my last life. If I die this time, I don't know if I'll wake up again—in Ametrine *or* in the real world.

My fingers curl into the dirt. If I die, my mom will never recover. My dad will spend the rest of his life thinking I hated him. I'll never get to go to Petey's soccer game like I promised. He would grow up without a big sister to protect. My throat squeezes.

I push myself off the ground, feverish with anxiety. Still, I force myself to breathe, to scan my surroundings. The herb section is on the south side of the garden, not too far from the guesthouse. That guesthouse has a kitchen. Drawers full of measuring cups, spoons . . . and knives.

I stiffen like a dog who's caught the scent. God knows I could use a weapon.

I creep through the garden, the stars hissing overhead. Shadows crawl over the ground, gutter between the trees. Where is Madison? Did she really disable her watch's tracking capabilities? It seems impossible that she would let me out of her sight. But then again, if I know anything about Madison, it's that she loves a good game. She doesn't only want to win; she wants to *play*. She must enjoy the cat-and-mouse of this.

Shouts drift over the property from every direction. The guesthouse waits at the edge of the garden, a small white colonial with shuttered windows. Its lights are off, a good sign. I grab the key from under a flowerpot, slit it into the lock, and push the door open.

I'm not making the same mistake as last time. No waiting, no hiding in the bathroom. Just get a weapon and get the hell out. I dart to the cupboard and yank it open. My hand wraps around the biggest knife I can find. I run my thumb along the edge, testing the sharpness.

"Bree?"

I whip around, brandishing the knife. Sitting, knees-to-chest, in the corner of the room, is Devin.

"No," I say, backing away. My back hits the counter. "No. I'm not falling for this again."

"Is that you?" His voice is small, raspy.

"Get the hell away from me." I point the knife at him, angle myself toward the door.

"No—please—" He flinches back, his arms raised in surrender. "It's not—I'm—I've been trying to find you."

"Right," I snarl. "And that's why you're here. Hiding."

"I'm not hiding! I remember you telling me about this place, how you'd have sleepovers here when you and Madison were kids," he says. His face twists with terror. "I thought you might end up here. God, Bree, are you okay? What have they been doing to you?"

My hands relax on the handle, just a little bit. "Tell me something only you would know."

His eyes soften. "Bree—"

"Do it."

He falls silent for a second. Outside, insects hum against the windows.

"When we first met," he says quietly, "it was just the two of us, in the art room. I told you a story about my old school, about the kids who bullied me. I told you about Joshua Greenwood."

The words sink in slowly. Joshua Greenwood. He had been the ringleader, the worst bully, the center of all Devin's humiliations. He punched Devin's teeth out in the bus lot. Stole his food, ripped his hair. He spread every rumor imaginable, outing Devin in the process. Devin hated talking about him. It was months before I learned Joshua's name.

Horrible relief rakes through my body. I lower the knife. "It's you."

His lip trembles. "It's me."

We crash into each other's arms. I bury my face in his neck and let out a sob. He holds me tighter, encompassing me in an impossible sense of safety.

"I can't get out," I whisper. "She locked my console, trapped me in the haptic suit. I tried to leave, but I can't. When I took off my goggles, I still felt everything they did to me."

Devin pulls back, eyes blazing. "What did they do to you?"

"I don't know how far Madison will take this," I say, dodging the question. "The pain is so real. I don't know what happens after I die this time. I don't have any lives left."

"Bree," he says. He hesitates for a second. "I—I have to tell you something."

Apprehension tightens my throat. "Okay." I don't like the look on his face, the fear in his eyes. "What?"

His hands clench and unclench. A spot on his cheek twitches as he begins to speak.

"When we got separated, I talked to an NPC," he says. "I was feeling awkward and didn't know who to hang out with, so I struck up a conversation with this guy at the dessert café. He was really interesting, and I went nerd mode, trying to understand how they work here. I was asking him about all kinds of things, and could feel him learning from my questions—the same way the HiveMind chat bots do. I think all the NPCs must operate from artificial intelligence. They have stories programmed into them, but they also absorb information in Ametrine, year after year. They've seen every one of Madison's parties."

"Okay." I rub my temples. "So?"

"I was asking them how to find you," he says. "They kept calling you Madison's special guest, and saying they couldn't interfere. I kept asking, using different phrases, trying to find a loophole in their programming. Through all of that, I learned that this 'special guest' model isn't new. Every year, Madison picks someone to torture. I don't know who she picked the first year. But last year was Kyle, and the year before that was someone named Amelia."

"*Amelia*," I repeat softly. "Devin, I—I think I saw her, in one of the simulations Madison brought me to. She was standing with a group of people, and there was blood coming out of her eyes. Then she disappeared. Why was she—"

Devin bites his lip. "Bree," he says.

"She left school after Ametrine," I say. "She dropped out. No one's seen her since."

"Bree," Devin says again. He closes his eyes, then opens them. "She didn't drop out."

He explains, fast and hushed, the best he can as darkness spreads through the house, clouds into my lungs. I jump at every sound, every shadow.

"Imagine that Ametrine is like a train, made up of connecting cars," he says. "Each car is a different location that the Pembrokes made for Madison. Where we are right now, that's one car. That New York–ish place we first landed in, that's another. They're all sort of lined up next to each other. Madison can use her watch to teleport between any of the different locations, but everyone else is limited to the car that Madison places them in. *Unless* they can find a portal."

"Wait, what?"

"For example," he says, "remember that sewer grate we jumped through? That was a portal from the New York fantasy world to the underwater club in the next 'car' over."

"Okay," I say. My head hurts. "But what does this have to do with Amelia?"

"Ametrine didn't always have portals," Devin says. "It used to be that each location was its own enclosed world, and the only way to switch between them was by using Madison's watch. Madison forced Amelia, alone, into one of those enclosed locations. The NPC said that this location was specifically designed to 'teach Amelia to be better.'" Devin grimaces. "Amelia had no way out, and Madison left her in there for hours. Amelia was so terrified that she—" He looks up to the ceiling, and for a second he seems unable to speak. "She went into cardiac arrest and died."

A faint ringing sound fills my ears. It feels like I've been plunged underwater, everything turning slow and dense.

Amelia's dead.

Madison killed her, here in Ametrine.

And she wants to kill me too.

CHAPTER 20

I MOVE TO THE COUNTER AND PICK UP the knife again. I study the serrated edges, my reflection cutting up at me. It feels better, holding this. Having some way to defend myself.

"I swear I've been seeing her," I say finally. "Amelia, I mean. Just—around Ametrine. When we first arrived, there was this girl standing next to the memory shop. And she was at the underwater club too. Watching me, frowning, looking creepy as hell."

Devin nods, his eyebrows furrowed in concentration. "You know how when people quit the game, their avatar stays behind until Madison gets rid of them?"

I think of Vanessa at the cliffside, how when she quit the simulation her body went limp and lifeless. Madison had kicked at the corpse, cursing, and zapped her away. *What a buzzkill.*

"Yeah," I say. "I saw that happen."

"Me too—some sophomore had a curfew."

Good. One less person hunting me. They'll have hell to pay next week, though, for leaving early.

"Usually when someone leaves their avatar behind, Madison can enter a command to delete the avatar, and then the body disappears," says Devin. "The avatars don't respawn again until the real person reenters the simulation. But since Amelia *died* in her suit, the simulation glitched and the signals got crossed. It's like she gave Ametrine a computer virus. And no matter how much they try to code over it, they can't entirely get her avatar out of the system."

"You learned all of this from an NPC?"

"Like I said, I asked him every variation of every possible question. Eventually I pieced it together," Devin says. "They call Amelia's avatar the Glitch. The other NPCs hate her. They think she's a traitor to Ametrine."

My heart swells. Leave it to Devin to manipulate an NPC's programming. Even when we got separated, he found a way to take care of me.

"If we want to get out, we need to think about this like Madison would. Like it's a game." A familiar glint sharpens in Devin's eyes. "We should start at the beginning: motive. What does she want and why does she want it?"

"She wants to hurt me, possibly kill me," I say. "At the very least, she wants to torture me in front of everyone. To punish me."

"Okay," says Devin. "Why?"

I think of what Madison showed me. Middle school Bree, running the school. Dancing with Mark. Spreading rumors. Gaslighting Madison, making fun of Madison, manipulating Madison.

I can't show him that side of me. Not now. What if he turns against me?

"I don't know," I lie. My teeth ache with tension. "She just... has it out for me."

He pauses for a fraction of a second. "What I can't figure out is how Madison has gotten away with it for so long," he says. "People don't even know Amelia's dead. How is that possible?"

"Maybe Madison is the only one who knows," I say quietly. "Madison and her parents. They'd help her cover it up. Amelia was by herself when it happened, so none of the other kids saw what went down. And if anyone *did* see, they could be sued into oblivion for breaking their NDA. Maybe the Pembrokes paid off Amelia's family, or threatened them, or—"

"We have to expose them," Devin says.

"We have to *survive*," I say. "How could we possibly prove any of this? I doubt an NPC's testimony would hold up in court. We'd need actual evidence, like a recording, or—"

My jaw goes slack. Of course. The highlight reel. Everything in Ametrine is being recorded. A sick, heavy feeling drops down my stomach. Because he's right. We have a responsibility to bring Madison to justice. And I think I know how.

"We need those recordings," I say. "And to get them, we need Madison's watch."

When we leave the guesthouse, another eerie silence has fallen over the estate. I have no idea where everyone's gone, if they're lurking nearby or searching for us in the surrounding woods, but miraculously, no one interrupts our sprint back to the mansion. The plants have started to wither, frost creeping up their stems. The sky swallows up its stars, leaving only blackness behind.

We sneak into the mansion through the back door. I tuck the kitchen knife into my belt and lead Devin to the basement stairs.

We don't turn on any lights, in case it would give away our location. I don't need the light anyway. I remember every corner, each dip of the steps. Devin takes my hand, and the familiarity grounds me, tightens a thread of courage up my back. This is Devin's hand. I know this hand like I know these walls, this staircase. I'm not alone. I'm in control again.

At the bottom of the steps, I pull Devin into the Pembrokes' theater room. My eyes have adjusted to the dark enough that I can make out the red cushioned chairs, the hulking projector.

"Watch my back," I whisper, and sink to the floor.

"What are you—"

"Shhh."

I scrabble at the rug, fingernails digging under one of the corners. I pull the rug up with a soft ripping sound, and there it is: A metal door in the ground. The entrance to Mr. Pembroke's bunker.

Devin lets out a low whistle.

Madison's voice creeps at the edge of my mind. *I feel like you're different around other people.* The two of us camped out in the bunker, thirteen years old. Madison picking at her thumbnails, avoiding my eyes. *Like you're not my best friend anymore. Or like you're trying to show off by being mean to me.*

Sweat prickles at my hairline. I push the memory back.

"Shit! It's locked." Devin yanks at the handle, panic fraying his voice.

That is so not true, I'd snapped back. Barely listening, trying to shut Madison up. *You sound crazy. Why are you always trying to start crap?*

I pull up the carpet an inch farther, revealing a camera and a tiny fingerprint scanner. Madison added me to their security system back in middle school, to make it easier to hang out there. If the simulation is based on that time period, then I should still be able to get in.

I press my thumb into the scanner.

Why do you even care what they think of you? You don't need them. We have each other.

The screen winks green, and the bunker door pops open. Devin glances at me, a strange awe on his face.

I ignore his expression, shame pressing in on me. I gesture to the open door. "Go ahead."

He presses a kiss to my temple. "You're brilliant."

My skin burns where he touched it. I can't find the words to respond, so I gesture again to the door. He jumps in.

Finally, I can turn on the lights.

The bunker looks exactly the way I remember it: Shelves

full of canned food, jugs for water, a sleeping pad, and a desk crammed with CCTV screens. A poster for the Isabella Stewart Gardner Museum is taped to the wall. My heart squeezes at the familiar logo. I'll never be able to see it without thinking of my dad, and those first days of spring when he would let Petey and me skip school to spend the day with him.

I head for the desk. All the security cameras are active, showing scenes from across the estate. Chet, yelling at some kid outside the garage. Mark, climbing up the mansion wall. Jake, passed out on the lawn. No sign of Madison and Everly.

Most importantly, the camera attached to the bunker door shows only darkness, its lens covered by the rug.

I log into the computer and open the bunker security app. All our old passwords still work. I delete Madison, her parents, and her grandma from the security settings. Then, since we're already inside, I delete my name too—just in case Madison would summon a clone to get in.

It's a pathetic act of caution. If she really wants to get in, she'll teleport. But knowing Madison, she'll want to play by the rules of her own game. She'll want to savor each challenge and enjoy watching me try to stop her.

"This should slow them down." I turn to Devin. "Are you ready?"

The plan is simple. Devin will exit the simulation. I'll hide his avatar body here in the bunker, where no one can see it and realize he's up to something. In the real world, Devin will open

Madison's console and steal her watch. He'll use it to unlock my console from the outside, and we'll get the hell out of there, evidence in hand.

Devin takes my hand and squeezes it. "I'm ready." He kisses my knuckles, one by one. Then he lets go and reaches upward, toward his invisible headset. "See you soon."

"*Wait.*" I seize his wrist. "Devin—wait."

He stops. "What? Are you okay?"

"I just—" I take his hands again. My throat aches. I need to tell him the truth. That I wasn't always the victim. That Madison, twisted as she is, has good reason to hate me. She doesn't have a reason to *kill* me, but—still. He deserves to know. What if I don't get another chance to tell him?

But his eyes are so gentle, so loving. He looks at me like he couldn't be more certain of my goodness.

"I'm sorry," I say. "I . . . I just wanted to say goodbye. In case."

Devin's hands tighten. "Don't talk like that."

"You were right from the beginning. We never should have come here. This is all my fault." Tears burn at the corners of my eyes.

Devin pulls me closer, leaning his forehead against mine. "I'd follow you anywhere," he says. "That's a choice *I* get to make."

A sob rips out of my throat. His hands slide around either side of my face, holding me steady.

"This is real," I whisper. "Right?"

"None of this is," Devin says. "Except for us."

We melt into each other, and I hold him until he goes limp in my arms.

I lower his avatar slowly to the ground, fighting down a flush of panic at the sight of his lifeless body. He's okay. He's fine. The real Devin is escaping now.

Still, I slide his eyelids shut. I tuck a strand of his hair behind his ear.

When we get out, I'll tell him everything. I'll come clean. And I'll show him, every day, that I'm different now.

THUNK.

Ice shoots through my veins. The sound came from overhead.

THUNK.

The ceiling trembles. I scramble to the security camera screens.

THUNK. THUNK. THUNK.

The rug's been pulled up, light streaming through the bunker-door camera.

THUNK. THUNK. THUNK.

The lens sharpens, coming into focus. Madison and Everly stand over the door, holding axes. Madison leans in toward the camera, her face wide and ghostly on the security screen.

"Thought you could hide from me?" she asks.

The hairs on my arms stand up. Everly swings her ax and smashes it against the door again. The camera lens fractures.

THUNK.

My body moves before I tell it to, yanking Devin's avatar toward the table. I shove him under and scrape the chair in front of him, hiding him as best I can.

THUNK.

Madison's wild laugh twists through the air. She loves this. The chase, the adrenaline. It's all a game to her.

THUNK.

The ax doesn't seem to be working. It's glancing off the door, the metal holding. Maybe it'll stave them off long enough for Devin to get her watch. Maybe—

But then Madison flicks her wrist, and Everly's ax disappears. In its place, a gleaming blowtorch.

"Shit," I breathe.

Everly grins. She takes aim. And with a roar of flame, the security camera goes black.

CHAPTER 21

MELTED STEEL DRIPS OVER THE WALLS. A GAPING hole stares down from where the trap door used to be.

Everly leaps in first, landing in front of me. I stumble backward, pulling their attention away from where Devin's avatar is hidden.

Madison drops down next to Everly with unnatural grace, birdlike. She surveys the bunker.

"Here you are," she says. "You've been missing the party."

My breath saws in and out. Cold, animal fear radiates off me.

Madison blows a thread of hair out of her eyes. She turns to Everly. "How should we deal with her?" she asks. "Kill her ourselves? Or throw her to the wolves? I've never liked getting my hands dirty."

"We still have to show everyone the video," says Everly.

"That's the finishing touch," Madison says, waving her hand in dismissal. "We show the video *after* we kill her in Assassins. You know that."

"What are you talking about?" I demand.

Madison raises one silver brow. "So impatient."

She exchanges a glance with Everly. A silent agreement flows between them.

"You know, Bree," Everly says, "everyone at this party has one thing in common."

"In fact," Madison says, "every person at every one of my parties has *always* had one thing in common. Do you want to guess what it is?"

"They're all psychopaths?" I spit.

"They're all victims," Madison says. "Of the special guest."

Dread claws up my chest. My skin tightens, claustrophobic. Everyone at this party is a victim . . . of me? What does that even mean?

I cross my arms to stop them from shaking. "What are you talking about?"

"We have it on video," says Everly. "You've shit-talked every single person at this party."

The words glitch, not sinking in. My classmates' faces flash through my head, both familiar and distant. I've shit-talked *every person at this party*? There's no way. How would they even know that, much less get it on video?

"Including your precious Devin," Madison says.

I feel the color drain from my face.

"You're lying." My voice trembles. "How could you possibly know who I've talked about and who I haven't?"

"My parents are VR geniuses," Madison snaps. "You don't think I have a way to track your communications?"

The realization sinks through me. "HiveMind," I whisper.

Her parents own that entire social network. The app is installed on every kid's phone at Lincoln Academy. It has access to my camera and microphone. Of course she could track me through it, she could track *anyone* through it.

She smiles, neither confirming nor denying.

My vision slips in and out of focus. This can't be happening. All these years, she's been monitoring me. Videoing me. Watching me. Tracking every word that came out of my mouth.

She remembers things that I don't, every piece of gossip that I spread in an attempt to fit in. She knows that I talked about Vanessa cheating on Chet, and Kyle upstaging Madison, and Mark failing his precalc exam, to anyone who would listen.

And worst of all, she knows that a year ago, when Devin first arrived, I tried to befriend someone in my English class by making fun of him.

Rage splits my vision, crowds out all my senses. Fine, yeah, I was lonely and trying to make friends. I didn't care what it cost, who it made me. All I wanted was to not be alone anymore, because *she* abandoned me. And now she wants to hold me hostage over it?

She can take anything from me. Anything she wants, except for Devin.

"Why are you doing this?" My voice rises. "Haven't you made your point? I know I was a bad friend, but it's been years, Madison. I know I'm not perfect. I talk shit like everyone else does. Why can't you get over it? Why are you *still* so obsessed with me?"

Madison flinches. Everly's eyebrows shoot up.

Tense silence coils between us.

Then she says softly, "You really want to know?"

"Madison," Everly warns.

My ex–best friend takes a step forward. "It's insurance. A way to make sure that no matter what happens to you, no one tries to save you. Here, or in the real world. No one will protect you or ever be on your side." A strange sadness clouds her eyes. "I know the real you," she murmurs. "Everyone else should too."

The heat in my chest withers, morphs into something small and cold.

She extends one hand to me. "I want to show you one last thing, before we finish," she says. "What do you say, Breezy? One more memory, for old time's sake?"

Her hand hovers before me, each nail a perfect shade of pink.

I force myself to think beyond this moment. Somewhere, Devin is breaking out, trying to get into Madison's console. I need to buy him more time.

Madison's eyes flicker. I lift my chin, refusing to show her how afraid I am. Then I take her hand, and we disappear, leaving Everly behind.

The scene resettles, pixel by pixel. I snatch my hand out of Madison's as soon as we arrive.

We're in the mansion's living room. Fairy lights flicker across the walls and piano notes drift out of a vintage record player. People in suits and cocktail dresses buzz around, clinking glasses and sampling tiny cakes.

It's a Pembroke investor party. One that was thrown back in middle school, before everything went down. I know this because standing by the open bar, beer in hand, is my father.

Seeing him here, like this, is the first time that Ametrine doesn't feel real. I haven't even let myself look at his picture in three years.

Dad leans against the bar unsteadily. His eyes slide toward me, and for a moment, it's almost like we see each other. Then he rubs at his scruffy beard and gestures for another drink.

"This way," Madison says.

She strides out of the living room, but I don't follow. I stand, rooted in place, staring at my father.

"Come *on*."

The world contracts, and we teleport to her bedroom. Cherry blossom wallpaper, the scent of Bath and Body Works candles. Middle school versions of Madison, Everly, and I lay sprawled on the floor. Madison scrolls on her phone. Everly and I examine each other's fingers, comparing manicures. All of us are wearing stuffy dresses picked out by our parents.

"Everly and I are bored," middle school me says. Her natural brown hair is plaited into braids that reach down her back. "Her mom is gonna drop me off at home. See you Monday?"

"Yup," middle school Madison says, not looking up from her phone.

Middle school Everly and I stand up, stretch, and head out. The door clicks shut.

Middle school Madison stays on the ground, scrolling on her phone for another few minutes. Tiredness glazes her eyes. After a while, she stands up and goes over to her dresser to check her makeup.

She pauses, noticing something.

I follow her gaze. My old iPhone lies on Madison's dresser, forgotten.

She picks it up. Weighs it in her hands.

What is she doing? I silently scream at my past self to come back, to remember her phone, but the door stays closed.

Middle school Madison runs her finger up and down the edge of the screen. Deliberating.

"You thought I was just your dumb sidekick," the real Madison says, beside me. "But you know I've never liked losing."

I glance at her, but she's zeroed in on the scene ahead of us. On her past self.

Middle school Madison unlocks the phone. She doesn't struggle with the code—we always shared them with each other. I lurch forward and read over her shoulder as she pulls up my father's text thread.

"Don't," I whisper, as if I can stop her.

She types.

Dad, can you come pick me up?

Everly and I got into a fight and she dropped me off in a bad neighborhood. Please don't tell Mom. She'll be so pissed.

No. No—

Please Dad, she writes. I need help.

She didn't. She wouldn't. She knew my dad was downstairs, so drunk he couldn't even walk straight.

Please.

She hits Send. My stomach bottoms out as shock spreads through me.

She carefully deletes each message off my phone, covering her tracks. She straightens her hair in the mirror, tucks my phone in her pocket, and leaves the room.

Before I can turn to the real Madison, we teleport back downstairs. My father is leaving, throwing out slurred excuses, staggering on his feet. My feet ache with the urge to run, to stop him. All these years, he tried to tell us. He sobbed from the police station, begged my mother to believe him. *Bree called me. She needed me.* I assumed, all this time, that he was lying. That he was using me as an excuse. Every day since, I've hated him for it.

But he hadn't been lying.

Middle school Madison watches him leave, then takes out her own phone.

"Hello," she says coolly, backing out of the room. She leans into the speaker, a smile working its way up her mouth. "I'd like to report a drunk driver."

I can't move. I can't speak.

Madison did this. *She* set my father up. Yeah, he was the one drinking, and he shouldn't have gotten behind the wheel. But Madison took advantage. She made him think that I was in danger.

The past version of me *finally* reenters the house, laughing about how she forgot her phone. Madison hugs her, makes a throwaway comment about how ditzy she is. Then middle school Bree leaves again, phone in hand. All of it a minor inconvenience, not worth remembering. She has no idea what's going to happen next.

I fell completely into Madison's trap. My whole family did.

Heat swarms my face, my eyes burning. Madison did this—she ruined our lives—all because of some petty, middle school drama.

The truth crashes over me, again and again, as I turn back to the real Madison. She watches my reaction with a dark hunger, her clear, sharp eyes fixed on me. Under her gaze, a strange looseness breaks through me. Because no matter how terrible I was in middle school, I would never sink this low.

Madison's mouth twitches, impatient. Waiting for me to respond. The thought returns, like a wave lapping against the shore.

I never would have done this. I wouldn't target Madison's family. I wouldn't risk people getting hurt. Yeah, I'd been an idiot. But I wasn't a monster.

"Well?" Madison whispers.

And I know she's waited all these years to tell me. To show me that she won, to make me see how she did it. She's planned for this day, longed all these years for this sublime moment of suffering.

And God, I can't help it.

I burst out laughing.

CHAPTER 22

"YOU THINK THIS IS FUNNY?" HER VOICE SHAKES with fury. She teleports us back to the bunker, but Everly is gone. It's just the two of us, standing in the ruins of our old hang-out spot.

"Come on, admit it," I say. "This is hilarious. You were so butthurt about my middle school stupidity that you got the *police* involved."

"Your alcoholic father is the one who—"

"You wasted all of your time in high school on me." My mouth splits into an arrogant smile. "You've invested thousands of dollars and thousands of hours into tracking everything I say. For what? To make a video? To turn people against me? You created an entire virtual world for me, just to make me suffer for shit I said back in *middle school*. For your own birthday party! Of course I think this is funny. This shit is hilarious."

"You're not the only one I've tracked," Madison snarls. "Every special guest in Ametrine got a video, got their own custom world. But with the others, I knew they could learn their lesson. We welcomed Kyle into our friend group after last year. We protected him, even when everyone found out he'd been talking about them for—"

"Protected him?" I repeat, laughing again. "You've got to be kidding me. Is that what you think about Amelia too? That you were *protecting* her while you tortured her? When you gave her a heart attack and *killed* her?"

Madison pauses for a microsecond, an undefinable emotion moving across her face.

"Yeah," I say. "I know about that."

"Amelia was in over her head." She speaks through gritted teeth. "She couldn't make it two hours in Ametrine. It's not my fault she's weak."

"You're so insecure that you'd rather control people than give them the chance to betray you." I step closer, shoving the security desk's chair out of the way. "You're not teaching people a lesson or giving people a good party. This—all of this—is you trying to protect yourself. Because deep down, you know we have good reason to talk. You are just as 'pathetic' as the rest of us."

Madison opens her mouth to respond, but nothing comes out. Her eyes widen, landing on something behind me.

I wheel around. Devin's lifeless avatar slumps out from under the desk. I accidentally exposed him when I moved the chair.

Madison reaches for her watch and flinches. "What the—"

It's gone. Her watch is gone.

"*Everly!*" she screams.

Which means Devin took it in the real world.

"*CHET! KYLE!*"

I rip off my headset.

CHAPTER 23

THE CONSOLE DOOR SWINGS OPEN AND I FALL through, landing at Devin's feet.

"*Bree*. Thank God!"

He's back in street clothes, clutching Madison's watch. Dizziness squeezes my temples. I spit out the mouthguard and it clatters on the ground.

"The watch?" I wheeze.

"Here." He presses it into my hands. "We need to go. *Now*."

"My suit—" I fling my headset to the ground. "Undo my haptic suit. In the back—"

He scrambles to unfasten it, yanking against the stubborn straps. It's halfway down my shoulder when Chet arrives.

He hits us from behind, so hard that it knocks the wind out of me. Chet's fist rams into my back and I crumple, elbows flying forward, my chin snapping against the floor. Devin smashes into the ground beside me. Stars shriek into my vision. Pain jabs down my neck, my shoulders. Chet is roaring something, the words hazy under the shock, and all I can do is clutch at the watch, covering it with my fingers, hiding it from sight.

Chet rips me to my feet. He seizes the front of my haptic suit and raises me into the air, an inch from his face. He tears the straps back into place, locking me back in. I struggle against him while Devin screams obscenities from the floor, but Chet's too strong, he won't let me go—

"Where is it?" Chet snarls. His spit sprays into my face.

I cringe back from him, stifling a cry. A vein visibly throbs on his forehead. I refuse to open my fist.

"I have it!" Devin yells. "I have the watch. Let her go!"

Chet lets me fall. I collapse at his feet, gasping.

"Okay," he says to Devin. "We'll talk. But Madison's not done with her."

Then he grabs me by the suit collar and drags me across the floor. Back toward the consoles. Toward Ametrine.

"*No!*" I shove him, bracing myself against the floor, but he doesn't stop.

Devin crawls to his feet, his face dangerously pale. "You want the watch?" he demands, backing up. "Then come and get it. If you don't, I swear to God I'll break it. I'll throw it off the balcony!"

Chet lifts me off the ground again, dangling me in front of my empty console. The glass door gapes open, a hungry mouth. I scream and twist and pain screeches through my haptic suit—I can't tell what pain is coming from Ametrine and what's coming from Chet—I can't think, I can't see, I can't—*I can't*—Chet shoves me backward—my back hits the glass and the door bangs shut—Devin is yelling something—the automatic lock slides back into place—the sound that leaves my mouth isn't human—and still, still, my fist is closed around Madison's watch.

I'm back in the console. Someone is hitting me in the simulation, bursts of pain spiking through the suit. Outside, Chet is turning toward Devin as Devin sprints toward the balcony stairs along the side of the room.

I open my fist and frantically tap the watch, but the screen is locked. PLEASE ENTER THE PASSCODE. What? It needs a *passcode*? How did Devin unlock my console in the first place?

My mind races. The watch must have been unlocked on Madison's wrist when Devin stole it from her and got turned off during Chet's attack. Now I'm locked out.

Four numbers. What are they? I try the code we used as kids, and the screen flashes red. Madison's old phone passcode. Red. Sweat pools on my forehead, drips into my eyes. Another wave of pain lurches through my haptic suit, and I convulse, yelling out. Outside the console, footsteps thunder up the metal stairs. Devin's reached the balcony now, Chet close behind. He's trying to buy me time to figure out the wristband, to unlock the console and escape. But it's not working. Nothing's working.

Come on, come on, come *on*. Four numbers. What would Madison pick? I enter combination after combination. The screen keeps flashing red.

Devin shouts something that I can't make out. I glance up just in time to see Chet lunge for him, shoving him against the railing.

"Devin!"

The watch falls from my hands. I slam my fists into the glass wall, shrieking for Chet to stop. Devin fights to get free, still shouting—Chet locks his arms around Devin's neck—Devin swings at him.

And then, with one fluid motion, Chet hurls him off the balcony.

As he falls, I reach for my eyes. I scrabble for another headset, as if I can turn this off, wake into another, realer world, one where this isn't happening. Because he can't be falling. That can't be my Devin, body crumpled midair, streaking toward the ground.

But my fingers meet only skin, the dampness of my own flesh. No pixels, no headset. Someone is screaming, the sound long and unending. And Devin hits the ground, his feet smashing into the hard floor with a horrible cracking sound. His wails of agony are real, too real.

"DEVIN! NO—*NO*—!"

I slam myself against the console walls again and again, so hard the structure shakes. My knuckles split open and blood smears against the glass, and it hurts so much it's blinding, but I can't get out, I can't get to him. His leg splays out at an unnatural angle, blood already soaking through his pants. He sobs something I can't make out, delirious with pain. Chet stands on the balcony, screeching with laughter.

I scramble to pick up the watch, sobbing, panic fraying every inch of my body. If I can just get this code—if I can just get out of this console—if I could just *get to him*—

My hands shake on the device, so hard I can't see the screen. My breath is shallow, jagged. There's not enough oxygen in here, not enough room to think. Is anyone else out? Can anyone else help Devin? I scan the rows of consoles, but everyone's grinning in their headsets, oblivious.

Then my eyes fall on Vanessa's console. The one that should be empty.

But it's not empty.

My mouth falls open in disbelief. Raw, numb shock vibrates through me.

My little brother, Petey, is in there. He's wearing a headset and haptic suit. Somehow, he's been brought into Ametrine.

CHAPTER 24

I FALL TO MY KNEES, COVERING MY FACE as if to shield against what I'm seeing. Am I hallucinating? How could Petey be here?

I look up again and fuck, *fuck*, it's definitely him. What is he doing? Why is he here? The shock morphs into horror, a feeling like bugs crawling up my throat, flooding into my mouth. *Madison*. Why did she bring him here? What is she doing to him?

Devin twitches on the ground, moaning in pain. I have to help him, and I have to get Petey out of Ametrine. *Now.*

It registers then, what I need to do. This watch is the only way to unlock my console, and Madison is the only person who knows the code. I have to go back in and rescue Petey. He can call an ambulance for Devin once he escapes Ametrine.

As for the code . . . I'll make Madison hand it over. Whatever it takes.

I don't give myself time to back out. I reach for the headset and disappear.

I respawn in the bunker, slumped at Madison's feet. Everly stands against the wall, arms crossed. She's leaning back, away from Madison.

"How fucking useless are you?" Madison says to her. "I thought you had eyes on Chet. Where is he? Why hasn't he brought back the watch yet?"

Everly's eyes slide toward me. Surprise flits across her face.

"I don't know why I bother with either of you," Madison spits. "Any time I give you a basic fucking task, you find a way to screw it up."

"Madison," Everly says.

"Don't interrupt me. It's so annoying when you interrupt me."

"But, Madison—"

"*What?*"

Everly lifts her chin, nodding in my direction. Madison glances down at me. I offer a weird, bland smile, to show her what she already knows: that I'm not a lifeless avatar anymore.

Madison's rage disappears. The red in her cheeks smooths to a pearly white. Her shoulders jerk back, straightening, as she feigns a sudden confidence.

"Well," she says. A smirk creeps up her lips. "Look who came crawling back."

I snake my hand into my suit pocket, tucking the watch out of sight. Madison still thinks Chet or Devin has it. I stand up slowly, trying to hide how much I'm shaking.

"Everly," I say, "you need to leave Ametrine right now, and call 911. Devin—"

"Excuse me?" Madison says. "Now you're giving orders?"

"Chet threw Devin off the balcony," I say, keeping my eyes on Everly. "His leg is broken, he's bleeding out, and I'm locked in my console. I know we're not friends, but—but from one human being to another, Everly, I need your help. *Please*."

Madison laughs, the sound ringing through the bunker. "You really think we're going to fall for that?"

Everly looks between us, uncertain. "Why was Devin on the balcony?"

"Chet chased him up there," I say. "If you don't believe me, you can go see for yourself. But please, he needs—"

"She's lying," Madison says. "Don't listen to her."

"I'm not lying, she—"

"She's trying to split us up. Turn us against each other," Madison says.

"No," I say, my voice rising, "I'm trying to stop *you* from *killing* another student!"

Shocked silence falls through the bunker. Everly's eyes widen. "What are you talking about?" she whispers.

"Shut up!" Madison shouts. The flush is back, climbing up her neck. "She's lying!"

"I'm talking about Amelia," I say, speaking over her. "I'm talking about the girl she tortured for hours, sophomore year. The girl who had a heart attack and died in here."

"Amelia?" Everly repeats. She glances between me and Madison, her eyebrows furrowing. "I thought she switched schools."

"She's dead," I say. "And Devin's going to die too if he doesn't get help."

"Liar!" Madison screams. She jolts forward, winding up to hit me, but I dodge the blow and jump up on the desk. The security camera screens scatter onto the floor. She turns, seething, back to Everly. "I need the watch. Where the fuck is Chet?"

"I'll go get him," says Everly.

"If that loser actually is hurt, don't call anyone. I'll deal with it later," Madison says. "And come straight back, as soon as you have the watch. Got it?"

"Madison—"

"Don't. Call. Anyone," Madison says. "Or we're done. Your scholarship is done. Your internship is done. Your *life* is done."

"I get it," Everly snaps.

She reaches for her headset. Our eyes meet for half a second, and then her body slumps to the floor.

The watch burns in my pocket. Without the code, my only advantage is that Madison doesn't have it. We're almost on a level playing field.

I can't trust Everly to get help. I need to find Petey. If I can find him and tell him what's going on, he can leave and call 911. My chest contracts. Unless Madison locked him in too.

I scrabble with my belt, pulling free the kitchen knife I'd taken during the Assassins game.

"Oh, cute," Madison says, regarding the knife. "Congratulations, Bree. You're *sooo* badass."

"I'm only going to ask you this one time," I say. I point the knife at her perfect bronzed cheekbones. "Where is my brother?"

Madison tilts her head to the side. "Your brother?"

"Yes, my *brother,* where's my fucking brother?" A knot squeezes in my throat. My voice comes out ragged. "Petey. What did you do to him?" Hot, traitorous tears press at my eyes.

Madison pauses, considering me. Then she laughs. "I have no idea where your gross brother is," she says. "He's not here, obviously. Why would I give *him* a spiral key?"

"Don't play dumb," I say, jabbing the knife at her. "I saw him in Vanessa's console."

"I didn't invite him," Madison says. "If he's here, it's because he followed *you.*"

Followed me? How would he do that? *Why* would he do that?

Then I remember our conversation last night, before the party. When he lumbered into the room, stinky from soccer practice, and asked why I was making a collage for Madison. *Don't we hate her?*

He wanted to see the invitation, to make sure it was real. He must have memorized the address and followed me here. Found Vanessa's empty console, her abandoned suit, and thought, *Why not?*

"Where is the spawning spot?" I demand. "Did he start in the city like the rest of us did?"

Infuriatingly, Madison shrugs.

"Show me where he is!" I shout.

"I *can't,* remember? Your boyfriend stole my watch. We can't teleport without it."

We can't teleport. But what had Devin said about Ametrine? That each location is lined up next to the other? Like a series of cars in a connected train . . .

Madison can use her watch to teleport between any of the different locations, but everyone else is limited to the car that Madison places them in. Unless they can find a portal.

Every location in Ametrine has a portal. Because of what happened to Amelia, there always needs to be a way out, as a safety precaution. Which means somewhere on this estate—possibly even in this bunker—there's a way out.

I jump down from the desk and start tearing through the room. I flip the table over. I throw each computer screen onto the ground. I rip up the rug and shake it.

"What are you doing?" Madison grabs me by the shoulder, but I jerk away. "Are you throwing some kind of temper tantrum?"

I pick up her dad's sleeping pad and fling it across the room. I run my hands over the bare floor, feeling for a secret entrance. Finding nothing, I turn to the walls. The Isabella Stewart Gardner Museum poster smiles down at me, and for a second I pause. My chest rises and falls. My heartbeat slams in my ears.

"You're really putting on a show," Madison says. "What, have you not gotten enough attention tonight?"

I had that same poster in my room as a kid. I got it from one of the annual trips my dad took me and Petey on. Cold lemonade, a day in the park, then geeking out at the museum. The first day of spring.

"Where the hell is Everly?" Madison hisses to herself.

I leap up and snag the corner of the poster. Then I rip it down, tearing half of it off the wall. Emotion pounds through my chest, flares along my nerve endings. This feels like a darker, violent version of making a collage. I keep pulling it off the wall in strips.

I stagger back, taking in the wreckage. A soft blue glow pulses beneath the final shreds of the poster. A portal.

I don't give Madison time to react. I pull the watch out of my pocket, fasten it on my wrist, and dive into the light.

CHAPTER 25

A CAR HONKS BEHIND ME. POLLEN ITCHES IN the air, nestles behind my eyelids. Under my feet, cracks sprawl over the sidewalk.

Familiarity stirs in me. I'm in Boston, standing on Evans Way—the road that leads to the Isabella Stewart Gardner Museum. Pink flags advertising the museum jut off the streetlamps. Up ahead, the museum building slides from brick to glass, angling pedestrians toward the entrance doors.

A crisp breeze rustles my hair. Goose bumps pucker along my arms. The trees lining the sidewalk sway, the leaves a pale and anxious green. The color of spring.

My hand drifts toward the watch. Madison loves visiting the city. Maybe the passcode is a play off one of Boston's zip codes? But before I can try it, a smear of blue materializes beside me. I jerk my hand back, angling the watch out of sight as Madison steps through the portal.

She lands beside me with an irritated huff. The portal swallows shut. She peers around, the pale sunlight crackling over her face. "Ugh," she says. "This."

There's no magical slant to this location. Ordinary NPCs pass down the street, kids drinking soda, parents lining up outside the museum. Why would Madison have such an unremarkable place programmed into Ametrine? Was this another potential torturing ground?

"Let's get out of here," Madison says. "This place is boring." Her voice is a straight line, perfectly casual. But her eyes flash from me to the museum, and back again. She's hiding something.

I take a step forward, and she slips in front of me. "I *said* we're going back," she says. "Now."

"Hang on," I say. Maybe I can bait her into giving me information—any insight could give me a hint to the passcode. "What is this place? It doesn't seem very Ametrian. Just some boring museum."

Her cheek twitches. I wonder if she remembers the stories I used to tell her, about coming here with my dad. "It's . . ." A strange pain moves under the surface of her expression. "I don't know. It must be some stupid addition my parents made."

Interesting. I look around again. As I do, she lunges forward and seizes my arm. Her eyes dart down to my wrist.

To the watch.

"You fucking bitch," she breathes.

Shit.

I yank my arm free, twisting out of her grip. She shrieks in fury, making another swipe at me, but I'm too fast. I dodge, shove her into the bushes, and sprint toward the museum entrance.

Startled NPCs cry out as I weave between them, barreling through the crowd and past the glass doors. Air-conditioning blasts into my face. It smells like Windex and floor polish. I burst through the lobby, veer past the ticketing desk, and push aside an angry employee at the coat check. My shoes squeak against the slick floor.

As I run, I try to unlock the watch, haphazardly typing every combination I can think of. Variations of Boston's zip codes, key words encoded to numbers, significant years in Madison's life. Nothing works. The screen keeps buzzing red.

Madison isn't far behind—she's screeching out threats from the lobby, her voice echoing off the walls. I turn down the Palace Corridor, racing toward the courtyard. Vibrant orange flowers curl along the stone walls, exploding into a full-on garden the farther in I go. Vines tangle along the pillars, and white petals frame the statues posing throughout the courtyard. The sharp floral scent fills my mouth, clouds my brain. It smells exactly like it did three years ago, the last time I came here with Petey and my dad. Azaleas and orchids, pinched with pine.

As if summoned, Petey's voice drifts through the courtyard. "Bree?" he calls. His tone is high and scared, like he's searching for a lost dog. "*Bree!*"

I skid to a stop. Every NPC in the courtyard stands still, staring at me. One child raises their hand at me, pointing. Madison's voice ricochets down from the hall, coming closer.

Petey. He's here.

I take off in the direction of his voice, streaking out of the courtyard and toward the stairs. Bright blue paint shines off the stairway walls, tapestries hanging off the corners. Muscle memory kicks in as I clear the steps. Petey's favorite item in the museum is a pair of metal bears, sculpted thousands of years ago in China. He used to stand at the exhibit for ages, marveling, asking Dad ridiculous questions. *Why are the bears sitting like that? What did they eat back then? Did they attack people? Can we get a bear statue for my room?*

I burst into the Early Italian Room. Bloodred wallpaper, gilded furniture, looming gothic paintings. And there's my little brother, stationed in front of the metal bear statues.

"PETEY!"

I dive toward him, flinging my arms around his neck. The NPCs near him scatter, murmuring in disapproval. I touch his hair, his shoulders, checking that he isn't hurt. "Petey, what are you doing here? How did you—"

"I was trying to find you," Petey says. "I've been looking everywhere."

"What? Why would you—"

"In case Ametrine wasn't safe after all," Petey says, as if it's obvious. "It's like I said at home. I've heard there's no rules here. Anything can happen."

"But you—"

"When I got here, nobody was around. Just a bunch of NPCs. I asked one of them what to do, and they said I could do *anything*, so I . . ." He lowered his eyes, embarrassed. "I asked to see the bears."

I stare at him, flabbergasted. He must have taken the commuter rail at night, by himself, and walked through the dark streets of Boston to arrive here. He saw Vanessa's empty console and strapped himself in, planning to find me. And after all of that, once he arrived, he got distracted by the *bears*. It's so classic Petey I can't even respond.

"I wanted to remember what it was like," says Petey. He scuffs his shoe against the floor. "You know. Being here."

The unspoken words hang between us: *Being here . . . with Dad.*

The simulation seems to shiver. Recognition sweeps through me, and a question curls in the back of my mind. Is this corner of Ametrine an exact replica of those spring days we spent with Dad? I'd told Madison about those visits. She knew how much they meant to me.

"I thought maybe you'd want to be here too," Petey says. His face shines with pride. "And I was right!"

My heart aches. I grip him by the shoulders and force him

to look at me. "Petey, listen. You need to get out of Ametrine, right now," I say. "You were right. It's not safe in here. I need you to leave your console and call 911. Madison locked me in my console, so I can't get out and do it myself. Devin needs your help. He's hurt in the real world, and I can't get to him."

"You're trapped?"

"Yes. Madison will catch up any second. She wants to hurt us. So I need you to go, right now."

Petey pulls away from me. "I can't leave. How am I going to protect you?"

Jesus Christ. How many times do I have to explain this to him?

"Petey." I try to wrestle my tone into something patient. "You don't need to protect me."

"Who's gonna do it?" Petey bursts out. "Dad's gone. You barely talk to Mom or Lex. Devin never comes over. You're all alone." His chin wobbles. Tears are building in his big brown eyes. "You're my sister. I *have* to protect you."

"That's not true," I whisper. I reach for his hand, but he cringes away, snot dripping down his lip. "Hey. Stop. I'm not all alone. And you don't need to be worrying about me like that. But right now, Devin's in a lot of trouble, more than I am. So I need you to go back and help him. Okay?"

"I have a better idea," Madison says.

I whip around. She stands at the entrance to the stairwell,

chest heaving. Sweat plasters her hair to her forehead. I step in front of Petey, shielding him from her. My hand moves to my belt again, where the kitchen knife is stowed.

"Don't worry," Madison says. "I'm not here to hurt anyone. I want to make a bargain."

"A *bargain*?" My fingers tighten on the knife, but I don't take it out. Not yet. "You've got to be kidding me."

Madison strolls into the room. She levels a glare at the remaining NPCs, and they rush out, muttering to each other, clutching their bags.

"You and I both know you can't get out of your console without the passcode," Madison says.

I don't reply. She steps closer.

"There's no other way out," Madison says. "No backup, no other programming. It's this watch, or nothing."

I track her as she circles us, shifting my body so I'm always facing her, always in front of Petey. Still, I say nothing.

"If you can't get out of your console, you can't help your precious boyfriend," says Madison. "So give me the watch, and I'll unlock it for you."

The watch burns against my wrist. Petey whimpers behind me.

"No way," I say. "If I give you the watch, you won't let me out. You'll just keep me here and torture me."

"I want this to be over as much as you do," Madison says.

I actually laugh at that. "How stupid do you think I am?"

"Believe it or not, you aren't actually that fun to be around." Madison's lip curls. "And besides. Every second you spend here is another second that Devin bleeds out." She traces the edge of a golden picture frame, then examines her finger as though checking it for dust. "That's the simple truth. So what are you going to do, Bree? Are you going to swallow your pride, or let him die?"

I cast a desperate look to Petey. *Will you please go?* But he shakes his head. The stubborn kid won't leave me.

"Madison! There you are!"

Everyone jumps. Madison swings around, turning to the stairwell entrance, where, of all people, her *parents* are walking through.

My fear turns into confusion. What the hell are they doing here?

Madison's mom radiates beauty. Her bronze hair falls in luscious waves down her shoulders. Her hexagonal glasses sparkle. But more than that, she seems . . . warmer than I remember. Madison's dad too. He's holding his wife's hand, something I've never seen him do in real life. Laugh lines crease the sides of his eyes as he grins.

Petey ducks out from under my arm. "Mr. and Mrs. Pembroke?" he says.

But they only have eyes for Madison. When Mr. Pembroke spots her, he cheers out loud. "There's my girl," he says, throwing his arm over her shoulder. He ruffles her hair. "We've been looking all over for you, kiddo. How are you enjoying the museum?"

Madison seems frozen in place. She opens her mouth, but no words come out.

"You invited your parents to your party?" Petey asks.

Mrs. Pembroke squeezes Madison's hand. I've never seen her parents give her this much affection. From what I remember, they barely spoke to her, let alone hugged her or touched her. They offloaded most of her care to Grandma Edie.

A quiet realization unfurls through my mind. "No," I say slowly to Petey. "Those aren't her parents. They're NPCs."

NPCs playing the role of Madison's parents. The type of parents she *wishes* they were.

It finally makes sense. This secret location in Ametrine—Madison's most private space, a location that's hidden inside a literal *bunker*—is an imitation of something I had growing up, that she wanted. A family that gives a shit. Parents who are imperfect, but try.

Her own parents created an entire alternate reality to keep her entertained, but didn't know how to make her feel loved. Madison wanted what I had. A mother who spent time with her, no strings attached. A dad who skipped work every first day of spring to take her to a museum.

Madison rips away from her parents. "Get off me!"

Mrs. Pembroke yelps, clutching her husband's arm. "Baby, what's the matter?"

Madison rounds on us, her face sheet white. “Hand over the watch,” she says. “I’m done playing games. Give it to me *now*!”

But she’s too late—I’ve figured it out. I flick on the watch and type in the date: *0419*. This year’s first day of spring.

This time, the screen turns green.

CHAPTER 26

IT TAKES LESS THAN TEN SECONDS. I ZAP Petey out of Ametrine, and his avatar crumples to the ground. Madison lunges toward me. Right as we collide, I yank off my headset.

The world spins, tightens. In Ametrine, Madison's fist slams into my jaw, and the pain radiates up my face. Then the colors rush back in, colors from the real world, and I tap SPECIAL GUEST, then UNLOCK CONSOLE on the watch, and the door unlatches.

I heave the door open and spill out, onto the warehouse floor.

"DEVIN!" I scream.

I fumble with the street clothes I'd left outside the console, trying to get my phone out of the pants pocket. Devin calls out to me, his voice slurring. I yank my phone out and dial 911. Petey jumps out of his console and runs up to my side.

"Holy shit!" he says when he sees Devin.

"Go get help," I hiss to him. "Find someone, *anyone*—and don't say the s-word, Petey."

"Shit! Shit! Shit!" he says, zooming toward the exit.

I grab my shirt and start toward Devin, thinking I can make a tourniquet of some kind, when I realize someone's beat me to it. A bloody rag is tied off just above his knee. Did he somehow do that himself, through the blinding pain? The phone keeps ringing into my ear, no one picking up. I glance down at the screen just as Madison's console door blasts open.

She steps out, still wearing her haptic suit. "Put down the phone," she says.

I stumble a step backward. "No way. I'm getting help."

"Give me the watch," Madison says, "and we can get this cleaned up."

The watch. She wants the recordings stored there—all the evidence of Ametrine's violence, filed safely away.

"911, what's your emergency?" A flat voice cuts into my flurry of realizations.

"Hello?" I shriek into the phone. "My boyfriend is injured. He got pushed off a balcony. We're at—"

Madison slams into me. We go down in a tangle of limbs. She knocks the phone out of my hand, and it skids across the floor.

"You—"

"Give me the watch!"

I kick her in the stomach, and she lurches back. I surge to my feet and run, weaving between the consoles. I throw myself against one of the empty ones and it wobbles, tilts, and crashes to the ground, drawing Madison to the sound. Then I sprint in the opposite direction and hide behind one of the other consoles.

I don't have long. The consoles are glass, and she'll spot me any second now. My phone lies faceup across the room, next to Devin. The 911 operator should still be on the line and able to track my call. They—or Petey—will send someone to help. I want to go to Devin right now—it's a physical, terrorizing want—but Madison is still after me. If I could just alert the other kids, get them to wake up and see Devin bleeding out, surely they would put a stop to this. Right? Fear pinches my chest. Or would they join in in our deaths, like they did during Assassins?

It doesn't matter—the other students are my best shot. And right now they're still deep in Ametrine, their senses trapped elsewhere. The only way to reach them is through the watch. I flick on the screen, trying to figure out how to end the simulation.

Devin cries out, and my thoughts disappear. "Help!" he calls out. "Someone, please—" It takes all of my willpower not to run to him.

How do you end the simulation? Where is the fucking button? I swipe through a thousand different useless commands.

"Bree!" Devin's voice rises to a scream. *"Bree, help me!"*

My body moves before I can stop it. I leap out from behind the console, straining toward him, and the second I do, Madison hurls into me. Her elbow launches into my nose. She grabs me by the hair and flings me to the ground.

I land on my hands and knees, a gasp slashing out my mouth. The tangy scent of blood splatters the air. My nose gushes, slicking my chin.

"BREE!"

I clamber out of her grip, dragging streaks of blood behind me, and try to rise to my feet. Pain explodes across my face as Madison kicks me again, forcing me back to the ground.

"You are so weak," she says.

Bile burns at the back of my throat. "Get off me!"

She presses her foot harder into my chest.

"An ambulance is coming any minute," I wheeze. "Do you really want to be attacking me when they get here?" I choke on a glut of blood. "The game is over, Madison. Chet could have killed him."

"But he didn't." Madison seizes me by the front of my shirt. "Devin could have tripped and fell. It's your word against ours."

"What would they think?" I whisper, nodding to the group of consoles. "If they knew who you really are?" I wheeze for breath, struggling against her grip. "If they knew about *Amelia*?"

She releases me, and the back of my head cracks against the ground. Stars burst across my vision.

"Give. Me. The. Watch!"

She punctuates each word with a swinging kick to my ribs. I twist onto my belly, trying to block the blows with my back. I curl in on myself and protect the watch. I need the recordings stored in there—proof of everything that's happened in Ametrine. I won't let her do this to anyone else.

She kicks me again, this time smashing into my right ear. The world fractures, sound ballooning then going distant. Still, I hunch my body around the watch, blocking it in with my shoulders. As she continues to kick me, I flick the watch back on and try, one more time, to end the simulation.

I navigate to the settings, the timer. Blood runs down my mouth and dots the floor. At the bottom of the timer, a blue link catches my attention. My saving grace. It reads END SIMULATION.

I hit the button.

CHAPTER 27

MADISON DOESN'T EVEN NOTICE. SCREAMING LIKE A DEMON, she keeps beating the shit out of me as the console doors open.

"You think you can beat me? You think you can win?" Her voice rises in pitch. "Give me the watch, Bree. GIVE IT TO ME!"

Blow after blow smashes into my head, my ribs, my legs. I stop resisting, weakness sapping my limbs, and she rolls me over onto my back. Blood spills down my chin, stains my sweater scarlet. A crowd of students gathers behind Madison, watching.

"Please," I gasp out to them.

Madison snatches the watch out of my hands and delivers a final kick to my face. Pain shatters through my head, squeezes the world into a pinprick. Behind Madison, Everly stalks forward. She raises her phone and points it at me, capturing the final humiliation.

"Please," I say again, my voice scraping louder. I point toward Devin. "Please—Chet pushed him off the—he needs—"

"Shut up!" Madison snarls, snapping the watch onto her

wrist. I've failed. All the evidence of Ametrine is back in her hands.

Everly moves closer, still holding her phone aloft. "Madison," she says. The other students murmur behind her. She pauses for a long moment. "Get away from Bree."

Shock drops through me. The whole scene slows, glitches, rewinds. Did I hear that right?

"Excuse me?" Madison says, whirling on her.

"I'm filming this," Everly says. Her voice like cold metal. "Get away from Bree. Now."

Another murmur passes through the crowd. Someone shrieks as they notice Devin in a pool of blood, half-conscious on the floor.

"You've got to be kidding me," Madison says. But her voice is less certain.

Everly's hands tremble on her phone. She speaks through gritted teeth. "I called an ambulance for Devin ten minutes ago."

My mouth drops open as I remember the tourniquet on Devin's leg. Did Everly—

"This has gone too far, Madison," she says. "We're not in Ametrine anymore."

"You little traitor!" Madison swipes for the phone, but Everly dodges, still pointing the camera at her. "Are you fucking serious?"

Madison whips around to the balcony, looking for Chet.

But he's gone. He must have fled while we were in Ametrine, escaping before the ambulance arrives.

Madison turns back to Everly, her voice dropping to a hiss. "After all these years, this is how you repay me?"

"Repay you for what? Your friendship?" Everly breathes hard. "For torturing *me* in Ametrine freshman year?"

I inhale so sharply that I choke on my own blood. *Everly* was the special guest freshman year.

She was the test run. Madison's right hand. She must have had her own gossip monitored, videoed, and thrown back at her. She must have lived every single day of high school terrified of going through it again.

Madison's hands curl into fists at her side. "You signed an NDA."

Everly lifts her chin. "You killed Amelia."

Gasps scatter through the group. Someone screams, a broken sound.

"Liar!" Madison's voice echoes through the warehouse. She gestures desperately toward the other students. "Everly and Bree are just jealous. They're trying to ruin Ametrine for the rest of us. Amelia changed schools. She's fine. Nothing. Happened. And besides, this isn't about me or Everly or Amelia. This is about us getting payback on *her*." She points to me, and I flinch back. "She's been talking shit about every single one of you for the last three years. I have it on video."

"And how did you get those videos, Madison?" Everly says.

Madison ignores her, tapping something on her watch. A hologram spins up out of the screen, displaying a projection of me. I start to sit up, making a swipe for the watch, but Madison shoves me down again, bracing her foot against my chest. A morbid silence steals through the room.

I know it's wrong, I know I have bigger problems, but all I can think is that Devin is going to see this. He's going to see who I was, before I met him. And he's going to hate me.

The hologram flickers. It shows me as a freshman, in the cafeteria.

Acne bulged on my cheeks. My secondhand uniform hung off my frame. I loitered by the vending machines, watching a group of kids from my art class sitting together at lunch. They cackled and passed around a vape under the table. I tucked a strand of purple hair behind one ear, pushed my shoulders back, and slid into a seat next to a girl with a mullet.

"Did you see Mark Sato's self-portrait?" I asked them, referencing our final project. "He's lucky he's good at sports. He might be the dumbest person I've ever met."

They offered forced laughs. I smiled with all my teeth. A few minutes later, they moved tables.

The video changes. Now it's me in gym class, trying to befriend someone in the locker room. "I heard Everly is sleeping with Samantha," I said, pulling on a sports jersey. "Samantha is a *senior.* Is that even legal? Honestly, someone should report those sluts."

Then it's me in the bus lot, talking about Kyle. "If I had that much acne, I'd light my own face on fire."

Me in the library. "I heard she had sex in the Lincoln pool. She's so easy it's not even funny."

Me in the courtyard. "I heard his mom gave him up for adoption, but no one wanted him."

Me in the hallway. "I heard she got pregnant just to stop him from breaking up with her."

How did Madison get such a vivid video of this? It seems impossible that all of this came from phone cameras and HiveMind. There are too many high angles, as if watching us from above.

As the video goes on, an angry sheen melts over the warehouse, twitches through the crowd of students. Scene after scene, comment after comment. All I can do is lie under Madison's boot, cringing away from my own past.

God, what was I thinking? Why did I ever think saying shit like that would buy me friends?

Across the room, Devin's voice breaks through the haze. "This is bullshit."

Madison stiffens. I strain against her, and she digs her foot harder into my chest.

Devin shifts on the ground, wincing. He clutches at his leg, shaking with pain, barely conscious. Yet he's speaking—he's standing up for me.

"These videos are obviously doctored," he says, voice blurry. "Bree would never talk about people like that."

Shame spreads down my chest, hot as blood.

A feline smile creeps up Madison's face. "Is that so?"

The video fades into a new scene. Now it shows Vanessa and me sitting in Mrs. King's junior English class. Not this. Any video but this.

I wrap my hands around Madison's ankle. "Madison," I whisper. "Stop."

"Shut up," Madison says. "This is your own fault. *You* did this."

A sob heaves through me. Because the worst part is, she's right. I did this. All these years, I coped with my loneliness by attacking the people around me. Now, everyone is finally finding out. Maybe I really did bring this on myself.

In the video, Mrs. King is at the front of the classroom, introducing a new student. Devin, seemingly immune to embarrassment, stands up straight in his Lincoln uniform. His long hair glistens in a bun at the base of his neck. He offers an awkward wave to the class.

God, he looks so young. I recognize the over-bright smile, the way his shoulders creep up toward his ears: he was trying so hard not to show how scared he was.

Tears scorch down my cheeks, gather in my ears. How was

there ever a time when I didn't love him? I want to reach through the hologram and wrap my arms around him, and tell him he doesn't always need to be brave.

But in the video, the past version of me leans over to Vanessa. "Why is he smiling like such a huge fucking loser?" the old me says, nodding to Devin. "People only transfer into Lincoln this late when they were put on the waitlist. Is he even smart enough to be here?"

The real Devin breaks through again. "*Stop!* This isn't—"

"What school do you think he came from?" Vanessa asks me in the video.

"Who gives a shit?" the old me replies. "I bet they're glad he's gone. He looks so pathetic up there, I'm getting secondhand embarrassment."

I want to die. I actually, literally want to die, watching this. Why the fuck did I say that? What did I possibly think it would earn me?

Sirens wail outside the warehouse. Relief washes over me. The ambulance is finally here.

Everly raises her phone again. "Tell them how you got those videos, Madison."

Madison cuts off the projection. She rips her foot off my chest and I spasm at the release, finally free. I crawl toward Devin, blood smearing behind me. I need to get to him. More than anything else, I need to get to him.

"Tell them," Everly says, as Madison steps closer to her.

They stand nose to nose. The other students raise their phones too, capturing the showdown.

"Tell them how you monitor everyone's private messages on HiveMind," says Everly. "How you record everyone's life through their phone cameras. Tell them how you planted bugs and cameras all throughout the school, just to make sure you didn't miss anything that the phones don't capture. Tell them about the files you keep on every single person at this party. Tell them just how far your obsession goes."

I reach Devin and grab his hand. Blood squelches between our knuckles.

He moans. "My legs," he says.

"I'm sorry." I kiss his hands, his cheeks, his forehead. "I'm so sorry."

"It wasn't real, was it? Those videos—you didn't—"

"I'm sorry," I whisper again, pushing a strand of hair out of his eyes. "I'm so, so sorry."

"Bree. No," he says, voice cracking. "Tell me she was lying."

I squeeze my eyes shut. It would be so easy, to say what he wanted to hear. To bury my past, one more time.

But Devin doesn't deserve that.

"She wasn't lying," I say. "I wish she was. But I—I have to own this. I can't pretend it didn't happen, because it did."

His eyes widen. "You mean—in all those videos, you were actually—"

The warehouse doors fling open, sirens screeching.

"You're just like the rest of them," he whispers.

"*No!* I was—I—" I scramble for the words. "I was lonely. I was lonely and angry and confused and—I never hurt anyone. Not to their face. Everyone hated me and I just wanted to—to connect with people, and I was doing it in a shitty way. It was wrong, and I stopped as soon as I met you. I'm not like that anymore. I swear."

I can't stand the look on his face, like he's staring at a stranger. The EMTs flood inside. Their radios crackle and they shout over one another as they haul in a stretcher.

"You know the best version of me," I say. "You helped *make* the best version of me. You reminded me that I don't need to impress the people around me. All the good shit that was already there, that I'd forgotten about myself, you're always helping me remember. You, of all people, know who I am. I need you to believe that."

He opens his mouth, but no words come out.

"Devin," I say.

He shakes his head, the tiniest motion. Even that seems to hurt him.

"Please." I fumble for his hand, squeeze each of his knuckles. "Say something. Say you forgive me. Tell me we're okay."

"No," he says.

He jerks his hand away. My whole body goes cold.

"Look at me, Bree," he says. "My legs are fucked. It hurts so much that I can't even *think*, and you—all you care about is that I forgive you?"

"No! Devin, please—that's not—" The EMTS are rushing toward us. "Let me come with you to the hospital."

"No," he says again. His next words come out choked. "You've done enough."

Then the EMT's are on us, surrounding him, lifting him into the stretcher. I stumble back as they carry him out. As they take him away from me.

Surrounded by the swarm of adults, Madison wrenches away from Everly and glares at her. Her face glows white with rage. "I'll deal with you later."

She flicks her wrist to Mark and Kyle, gesturing them to her side. Neither one of them moves.

"Come *on*," she says. Her hand jerks toward her watch, like she has the urge to teleport them.

Mark shakes his head. "Nah, man," he says. "I didn't sign up for this."

Kyle turns to Everly. "Send me the video," he says. "I'll post it too."

"Don't you *dare*," Madison shrieks. "Kyle, I swear to God if you don't come with me right now, it's fucking over. Chet will post the video of you pissing your pants, and everyone will see that you're a pathetic little shit who can't even—"

"Fine," says Kyle. "More evidence against Ametrine. Against you. I'm done, Madison. I don't care anymore."

"I can make your life hell," Madison says. "Forget about my parents' recommendation letter. Forget about performing arts college. Your broke-ass family can't do shit for you. Your future goes down the drain, right now, if you don't—"

Mark steps in front of Kyle, blocking him from Madison's fury. He crosses his arms, biceps flexing. "He said he's done."

Madison's practically hyperventilating. She spots me and raises one shaking finger. "You did this," she says. "I won't forget."

Then she turns away and runs for the exit—alone.

CHAPTER 28

WHEN PETEY COMES BACK TO THE WAREHOUSE, HYSTERICAL and with a concerned bystander in tow, I send him home in a cab. He protests, demanding to stay with me and go home together, but I practically body-slam him into the car. The neighbor offers to pay the fare, and I'm too broke to argue. I can't have Petey here for another second. I need some space to breathe. To process the enormity of what happened.

I go back into the warehouse and strip off my haptic suit. The suction cups detach with a squelch, leaving behind angry red circles. The air-conditioning grazes my bare skin as I pull on my street clothes.

The EMTs want to take me to the hospital, want to do brain scans and treat the gashes in my face, but we don't have health insurance. No way am I making my mom pay for this. Things are tight enough as it is.

So I sit on the steps outside the warehouse and listen to the ambulance as it howls down the street, carrying Devin away with it. The distance stretches between us like a rubber band, tensing tighter and tighter. I bury my face in my hands.

Morning sunlight carves down the street and stains the buildings orange.

"You should have gone with them."

I don't look up, don't move my hands from my face.

Everly's vanilla perfume wafts over as she sits down next to me. "You probably have a concussion at least," she continues. "You need to get checked out."

I run my fingers along the dried blood on my temple. Pain spikes out under the touch. "I'm fine," I say.

She sighs, a long and tired sound. Silence hangs between us.

"Thank you," I say, after a second. "For calling the ambulance. And the tourniquet. How did you even know how to do that?"

"First aid class," Everly says. "They require it for my babysitting certification."

"Thank you," I say again. I don't say anything else.

Everly fiddles with the pearls around her neck. "Kyle posted my video on his HiveMind," she says. "His musical theater account, that everyone followed after *Cabaret* last year. The whole school will see it. They'll know about Devin and—" She closes her eyes for a second, wincing. "And Amelia. We're sending it to the school administration too."

I don't say anything. For a moment, we sit in silence, listening to the city wake up around us. Car horns blare down the street. Lost seagulls complain over the traffic.

Finally, I raise my head out of my hands. "Why did you do it?" I ask her.

Everly presses her lips together. She gazes ahead, still watching the city. "Which part?"

"Standing up to her," I say. "Finally saying no, after all this time."

"I . . ." She shakes her head. Scrubs a smudge of eyeliner off her face. "I know what it's like. Being punished by Madison."

The sun inches up in the sky, cutting through the autumn chill. She hugs her arms to her chest. What did she go through, as Madison's special guest freshman year?

"This isn't who I am," she says. "I'm tired of being afraid of her. I'm tired of doing everything she says, just to stay on her good side." She lowers her eyes. Her next words come out pinched. "I'm tired of loving her."

My heart squeezes. All these years, Everly has stayed at Madison's side. Even when I constantly tried to push them apart, Everly remained steady.

"I'm sorry I was so awful to you," I say.

Everly shrugs. "It was middle school."

"Yeah, but—still." A gust of wind hits us, lifting my hair off my shoulders. "I was jealous. You and Madison were so close. I didn't know I was bi yet, and I had all these weird confusing feelings like you were going to take her away from me."

Everly laughs under her breath. "You should not be the one apologizing."

"Well, I am."

She nods, once. We sit with that.

"I never thought of myself as the bad guy," Everly says. "Even when we were in Ametrine, I—I somehow didn't believe it. Like, at least I felt guilty, so that meant I wasn't a bad person. Every once in a while, I would talk Madison down from some sadistic idea, and I'd feel good about myself. Then I'd go join her for everything else she was doing." She shakes her head. "I thought I was being loyal. A good friend. But I was scared all the time. An actual friend would have stopped her sooner."

I don't have a response for that. She's right—what she did wasn't okay. I'm not forgiving her anytime soon.

"I thought I knew who I was." Her throat bobs as she swallows. "But I didn't. I—I still don't."

When I meet her eyes, I see myself shining through them, familiar but distant, a reflection of a reflection. Like when you stand in a corner of mirrors and see a different angle of your face than usual, a glimpse of accidental wholeness, and you think, *Is this how other people see me?*

It's easy to do things that contradict with who you are. Or, even, who you *think* you are. You can walk around believing you're one type of person, and then act entirely like another, without even realizing it. You can get so wrapped up in the story you tell about yourself. I did that for years.

Does Madison think she's a good person? When she sees the video Kyle posted, will she feel the shame I felt when she brought me into our middle school flashbacks?

My thoughts rip and layer over each other, an ever-shifting

collage. Madison is abusive. Manipulative. Vengeful. But maybe in her own twisted way, she's been trying to do something any good friend should do: hold her friends accountable to who they think they are.

Or maybe she's just an evil fucking psychopath. Maybe she enjoys the fear, the violence, the game.

Can both of these things be true at the same time?

"Go to the hospital, Bree," Everly says, standing up. "My parents will pay for it." She brushes off her gown and goes back inside.

I stay, sitting on the steps for a long, long time.

CHAPTER 29

MY MOM CRIES WHEN SHE SEES ME. SHE reaches for my face, then hesitates, as if she's scared she'll hurt me further. Then, unable to stop herself, she grips me by the chin to turn my head from side to side, examining every aching angle.

"I'm going to kill them," Aunt Lex says. She clutches the back of a kitchen chair, knuckles white. It looks like she wants to throw it across the room.

Petey sprints around the house in circles, yelling out every piece of the story he knows. Sweat plasters his hair to his forehead. His eyes have the wild, reeling look of a panicked horse.

"You went on the *train* like this?" Mom says, voice breaking. "Bree, if there was ever a time to call a cab—"

"We don't have the money for a cab," I say, trying to push past them.

"You put *me* in a cab!" Petey shouts.

"You could have called us," Lex says. "You *should* have called us. What were you thinking?"

"You need to sit down," Mom says, "and tell us what happened. Right now. Who did this to you? Petey was saying something about Madison?"

I don't want to talk to them. I don't want to see the pity on their faces, their righteous anger. I just want to take a shower and melt into bed. Try to forget that the last twelve hours ever happened.

Instead, I brace my hands on the kitchen table. "I need to talk to Dad."

"You need to *what*?" Mom squawks.

Petey materializes behind her. "What's Dad got to do with it?"

"Petey, go to your room," Lex says.

"No! I'm part of this. I was there. I should get to know what's happening. Mom—Mom, what's—"

In one swift motion, Lex picks Petey up—all five feet and four inches of him—and swings him over her shoulder. He kicks and screams like a child.

"Bree could have died in there!" he howls. "She could have *died*!"

He dissolves into sobs, pounding his fists into Lex's back. Lex carries him down the hall to our shared room and closes the door behind them.

Mom sinks into a chair at the kitchen table. Wrinkles curl out under her eyes like spiderwebs. God, she looks so old. If she was brought into Ametrine, those wrinkles would unravel into smoothness. The image growls behind my eyes: My mom, but younger, glowing, trapped in more favorable pixels. Her graying hair rich and shiny. Warmth in her cheeks. I blink and try to unthink it.

"Bree," she says. "You can't come home hours later than you said you would, looking like someone beat you within an inch of your life, and not tell me what's going on. We've got to get you to a doctor, and you have to tell me what happened."

She's right. I need to explain myself. But it feels like there's a knife in my throat.

I sit down next to her. She lays her hand on top of mine.

"The night that Dad got arrested," I begin, "I left my phone at Madison's house."

Everly was right. Madison gave me a concussion, bad enough that I have to stay in bed and off screens for a week. The doctor's orders are ridiculous. I'm supposed to rest but avoid sleeping, stimulate my mind a little but not too much, listen to podcasts but avoid reading. It's a medically approved purgatory.

I only break the screen rule once a day, to send Devin a message and check if he's messaged me back. While I wait for him to respond, I burn with anxiety. I twist in bed, hating every cell in my body, resenting every version of myself I've ever been.

Sunday, 9:00 AM

I'm so sorry, for everything. You were right—I can't believe I was so self-absorbed. All I want is for you to be okay. I'm thinking of you. I miss you. How are you feeling?

Read 10:02 AM

Monday, 7:02 AM

Hey. I just wanted to check in—are you still at the hospital? I love you.

Read 7:05 AM

Tuesday, 8:00 AM

Listen, I get it if you need some space, but I don't know what to do with all this silence. I'm so worried about you. Can you please let me know where your head is at? Please, whenever you feel up to it, call me.

Read 12:22 PM

On Wednesday, I finally take his silence as its own message. I stop texting him. But still, my thoughts won't let up. The obsession tightens like hands around my neck. Is he okay? Who is taking care of him? Has his mom stopped drinking long enough to realize her son needs help? Does his dad even know what happened? How is he eating, showering, moving with this injury? Who is he talking to? What is he thinking about? Does he miss me? Does he hate me? Is he going back to Lincoln? Will I ever get to see him again?

The anxiety is made worse by having so little to do. I can't watch TV, scroll through social media, or read. I start collages but lose interest before I finish them. A constant headache crowds behind my eyes. Devin is the only person at school who has my number and I deleted my HiveMind account, so I have no idea what's happening at school. What are people saying? How many people have seen the video? What do people think of me now? I spiral for hours, an audiobook droning in my ear.

And then there's my father. When I told him what Madison had done, he didn't speak for nearly thirty seconds. I clutched the phone, hand trembling.

When he finally responded, it came out choked. "I'm so sorry, baby," he said. "All these years, you thought I—you thought I was—oh, sweet pea. I'm so sorry." Another pause, the sound of him breathing. "Do you think we could see each other in person? Talk it through together?"

No. It was immediately too much. I spat out an excuse, hung up, and paced around the house, chest burning. A thousand conflicting emotions wrestled through me. Mom followed me into my room and sank down onto the bed, sitting at the edge like she did tucking me in as child. I paced around for a few more seconds, then collapsed next to her.

"It's not that I don't want to forgive him," I burst out. I pulled a pillow into my lap and tugged at a loose string in the pillowcase. "I want to be able to put it behind me. I want to be like you and Petey and Lex, and just, like—let it go."

Mom nodded, listening.

"I miss him so much. I want to be over it. But I'm just . . . I'm not."

"No one is expecting you to get over it," Mom said. She folded then refolded her hands in her lap. "I'm certainly not. None of us are, really. Just look at Petey—he's so high-strung, I don't know what to do with him. Aunt Lex gets so mad she can hardly talk. No one's asking you to forgive him, or forget what happened. No one's asking you to let go."

"I just—I feel like, now that I know the truth, it should change things. Now that I know Madison is the reason—"

Mom hummed and shook her head. "That girl is not the reason your father did what he did that night. He never should have gotten in that car after drinking. That was his decision, and it was the wrong one."

"But he thought I was in trouble. He thought that I needed him."

"Then he should have called me. He should have called you a cab. He should have done anything else, but he didn't," Mom said. "Baby, that's not your fault. That's not even Madison's fault. It's his. And that doesn't mean he's a bad man, or that he's not worthy of forgiveness. But it does mean he has to face the consequences of his own decisions."

"How do you do it?" I asked her.

"What, baby?"

"How do you still see him and talk to him without being angry? How have you forgiven him?"

She ran her tongue over her lips. Her eyebrows curved down as if in concentration. Then she lifted her shoulders in a helpless shrug. "I see who he's trying to become," she said. "Despite everything, I trust him to keep moving toward becoming that person."

So, I set boundaries. I don't meet up with him in person, but I talk to him on the phone at seven each evening. I ask about his new apartment, his AA meetings, the dog he adopted. It hurts, but it feels good at the same time because I know that I'm trying. We're trying. I tell him about Ametrine, the world Madison stole and then used against me. He shares stories about his own childhood best friend, and I listen. Maybe by the time the first day of spring comes around, I'll be ready to go to the museum with him and Petey.

I talk to other people too. Lincoln requires that I meet with the school counselor twice a week. The Headmaster asks for a statement on Chet and Madison. I learn that an investigation is being opened into Amelia's death.

On Friday, I break down and call Devin. The line rings and rings, but he never answers.

For the last week, Petey hasn't been sleeping well. He wakes in a panic several times a night, yelling out for me, terrified that I'm in danger. Mom and Aunt Lex have been sleeping less too, convening in the kitchen past our bedtime and talking in low, urgent voices. Tonight, when I go into fill up my water bottle, they fall silent. Aunt Lex crosses her arms and watches me. Mom picks up her mug, then sets it down again.

I turn on the tap and angle my bottle under the faucet. "What?" I demand, when they still don't say anything.

"You're up late," Lex says.

The water sloshes up to the rim. I pour the excess back into the sink and screw on the lid. The two of them exchange glances.

"*What?*" I say again.

"You should go to bed," Mom says. "It's almost eleven."

"I was about to."

Lex's phone lies faceup on the counter between them, the screen glinting. Mom's eyes flick to the phone, then back to me. It's playing a video with the sound off.

"What are you guys watching?"

Lex reaches for her phone, but I'm faster. I snatch it up, and the screen greets me with a live news feed from NBC Boston. A white guy with a swoop of blond hair stands in a navy-blue suit, clutching a microphone and standing outside of—wait.

"Is that Lincoln Academy?"

"No screens," Lex snaps, yanking it out of my grip.

Mom pinches the bridge of her nose.

The air is too thin all of a sudden. I can't breathe in all the way. "What's going on? Is it about the Pembrokes?"

Lex holds the phone against her chest. She looks to my mom for permission.

"The girl who died—her parents came forward," Mom says.

A distant panic builds in my body, like a storm gathering over a lake. But I have to stay calm. I have to seem okay, or else they won't tell me anything. "Let me see the phone."

"Please, baby," Mom says. "Go to bed. We can talk about it in the morning."

"No. I want to know what's happening." My voice comes out steady, a straight line. "If you don't show me, I'll look it up myself. I deserve to know. At least let me *listen* to the video."

Lex sighs. Mom leans into the counter, bracing herself on both elbows, her head bowed down. Lex turns up the audio.

. . . at the private academy where the victim went to school for two years before dying at a friend's birthday party. Witnesses have confirmed that the young woman died of a heart attack while participating in an exclusive demo of Pembroke

Technology's virtual reality game, titled "Ametrine." The exact contents of the game are unknown.

Following her death, the victim's parents allegedly fled the city, and have now come forward claiming that Pembroke Technology violently threatened them into silence.

Lex scoffs. "Your kid gets killed, and you stay quiet? What threat could ever be enough to convince you to do that?"

But she doesn't know the Pembrokes. She doesn't know how far they'd go. Maybe they threatened the other kids in Amelia's family, her siblings.

Lincoln Academy has been accused of illegally collaborating with Pembroke Technology to install private hidden cameras throughout the school, which have been used both for student discipline on the school's part, and to collect imaging data for Pembroke's AI-generated virtual reality game system.

The audio fizzes, then switches to a different newscaster.

Essentially, a new voice says, *Pembroke Technology uses artificial intelligence to create vibrant, detailed imagery in their games. For AI to generate accurate images, though, it needs to be fed images to work off of. The cameras installed throughout the Academy would help provide this—particularly if the game needs accurate renditions of the students who attend.*

If I might speculate, it seems possible that this was a mutually beneficial endeavor. The Academy got a state-of-the-art security system free of charge, and Pembroke Technology got a wealth of imagery for their games.

Thank you, Ted, the first voice says. *Pembroke Technology has also been accused of linking its social media platform, HiveMind, to these AI systems—meaning any data shared on that platform may also have been used to program the deadly VR game. This is a developing story. Stay tuned for live updates.*

"Jesus Christ," says Lex, turning off her phone.

Mom points to me. "Delete your HiveMind account."

"Already done." Honestly, I kind of want to throw my whole phone in the ocean. At least now I know how Ametrine was so accurate. Any detail I shared with someone on HiveMind, or at school—it was all being fed into Ametrine. My words, my photos, my life, spliced apart and repurposed.

All this time, I thought I'd been alone.

The door looks the same. Tall, polished wood, with the black handle I've turned a thousand times. I shift my weight from foot to foot. The sun pricks against my eyes. Everything has seemed too bright since I left Ametrine, another one of my concussion symptoms.

I ring the doorbell again. A bag of Cheetos crinkles under my arm.

Finally, the door jerks open. Devin's mother stands before me in stained sweatpants, holding a glass of wine.

"What?" she says.

A cold feeling moves through me at the sight of her, like a downdraft before rain. "I'm here to see Devin," I say. "Is he home?"

She scoffs. Dark circles flex under her eyes. "Where else would he be?"

She steps back into the house, and I follow her inside. A dank, sweaty smell hovers in the air despite the smooth walls and expensive furniture. Devin's mom slouches back to the living room and collapses on the couch.

"Don't get pregnant in my house," she says, and closes her eyes.

I weave through the dirty laundry strewn in the hallway and arrive outside Devin's bedroom door. My fist rises to knock. But I freeze there, hand aloft. What am I about to walk into? How pissed is he going to be that I'm here? He hasn't called all week. Is he trying to ghost me? To break up without actually saying goodbye? He wouldn't do that, right?

My spine straightens. I wipe my hands on my jeans. If he wants to break up, then he at least needs to say it to my face. I deserve an ending that does justice to what we had.

I need to do this.

I knock, three times. His voice drifts out, inviting me inside. I steel myself, and open the door.

"Bree?"

I face the door as I close it behind me, trying to gather my composure. Then, after a moment, I turn to face him.

He lies on his back in bed, both legs propped up and wrapped in casts. His hair sticks up in all directions, fuzzy with disarray. My chest contracts, a physical pain pressing against my rib cage. Devin. My Devin.

"You're here," he says.

My hands sweat against the Cheetos bag. "I—I know you might not want to see me."

He sits up a little, wincing as his legs adjust. I rush to his side and help him, a little shock zinging up my hands at the contact. God, I've missed him.

He studies me as I pull away. A blush grazes up my cheeks. I hand him the Cheetos bag.

"I . . . um." Why am I so shy all of a sudden? I swallow, try to wrestle my expression under control. "I brought you these. Figured you could use some comfort food."

"You trying to bribe me, Benson?" he says.

His tone seems encouraging, but I can't bring myself to smile. My fingers itch with the urge to touch him, to brush the hair out of his eyes, to trace the edge of his jaw. I want to make sure that every inch of him is still intact.

"Joking," he says. "Sorry. I—I don't know how to do this."

"How to do what?"

He lifts his shoulder, uncertain.

He's going to give me a heart attack. I cling to his words, a thousand different interpretations fighting for attention. But before I have the chance to ask, he changes course.

"How are you doing?" he asks.

Oh, God. Small talk.

"It's—it's been pretty shit," I say. "Madison gave me a concussion, so I've been off screens for the last week. No social media, no TV, no reading. Just . . . thinking."

"Same," says Devin.

"Are you going as insane as I am?"

"Possibly even more so," he says, nodding to his legs. "What with the excruciating pain and all."

"Fuck, I'm so sorry," I burst out. "I can't believe—"

"You didn't push me off that balcony."

"But I—"

"Stop."

Terror seizes every cell of my body. Is this it? Is he about to break up with me? I try desperately to gauge his expression, but I'm too panicked to get a good read.

"Is your mom taking care of you?" I ask him, diverting. "Are you getting everything that you need?"

"She's . . . being herself," Devin says. "She hasn't disappeared yet, so I'll take that as a good sign. I order takeout and she brings it to me from the front door. A true hero."

I rub the inside of my wrist. A headache presses up against

my temples. “Anything that you need,” I say, “I want to help with. It doesn’t matter what it is. I’m here for you. Okay?”

His eyes flick down, avoiding mine. “Tell me how you’re doing,” he says. “Are your folks holding up all right?”

“They’re—they’re fine.” My vision blurs. “Devin, I—”

“What?”

I can’t do this anymore.

“Are you breaking up with me?”

His eyes shoot back up to me. He opens his mouth, then closes it. Panic flames through me. I wobble a step back, scrabbling for composure. My tongue scrapes against my teeth, chalk-dry.

He drops the Cheetos off the side of the bed with a crinkling crash. “Bree—”

“Because if you are, it’s okay,” I say quickly, but my voice cracks. Flames press up my throat, rage behind my eyes. “I’d understand. I won’t hate you. But I—I need to know, because I love you, so, so much, and I’ve been going insane this week not hearing from you. Not knowing if you’re okay. If we’re okay.”

“I know,” Devin says. “I know. Me too.”

I clamp my mouth shut, biting back a sob. He looks so beautiful, even with the sweat on his forehead and the frizz in his hair.

He reaches out for me, and I draw closer, taking his hand in mine. “I’m not breaking up with you,” he says.

Relief sags through my entire body. He squeezes my hand and I squeeze back.

"You don't hate me?" I say. "For all that shit I said in those videos?"

"I've been thinking about it a lot," he says. "Like I said, I've had plenty of time to just, um, think this week. And no. I don't hate you for all that stuff you said. I could never hate you."

"Then why did you ghost me? Why haven't you answered any of my messages?"

He reaches up and brushes his knuckle against my cheek. "When I said I don't know how to do this," he says, "I meant I don't know how to . . . how to not run away. I know I've been distant. But that's not because I'm running away. It's because I'm trying not to."

I press my lips to his fingers.

"I was confused," he says. "And angry and hurt. Watching those videos, it felt like you'd betrayed me somehow. Then my legs were fucked, I was in total crisis, and it still felt like I was supposed to comfort *you*, instead of the other way around. The whole dynamic screwed with my head. I had sort through it on my own."

A thousand excuses rush to my lips. *I couldn't comfort you because you wouldn't let me in. I was in crisis too.* But I hold back. I try to absorb what he's saying.

"And about those videos," he says. "All of that manipulation you were doing, all of those shitty comments—it was triggering to see, but that was before I knew you. I fell in love with the person you are now. The art dork. The smart kid with the sharp mouth. I needed some space to remember that." A sad smile edges up his face. "Besides. How many times have I talked shit about Madison? I know it's different, but we've all been there. Sometimes gossip is a way of surviving. A way of knowing that you're not alone."

I wrap my arms around him and lean in. His warm, familiar smell folds over me like a blanket.

"I'm sorry I disappeared on you," he murmurs.

I nestle into the crook of his neck. "I'm sorry too. For everything."

We hold each other. Slowly the tension in my body unwinds. The voices in my head screaming HE'S GOING TO LEAVE YOU! ease down to a sputter. I genuinely understand where he's coming from, and I make a silent commitment to remember this.

"I love you," I tell him. "You're so good to me."

His hands knot in my hair, pull me in closer. Like he wants us to merge, to dissolve into each other.

"I love you more." He pulls back. "This is real. It's you and me."

I breathe out, all the way. "It's you and me."

It isn't easy now, knowing whether things are real. Sleep has become a battleground. Dreams are too similar to Ametrine—

the shifting characters, bending space, all the infinite possibilities for violence. I keep dreaming that I'm in there again, that I can't get out, that Madison is coming for me, and when I wake in the too-cold room with Petey whimpering nearby, it takes me entire minutes to realize I'm safe, I'm home, it was only a dream.

And that's just at night. During the day I've been followed by horrific, all-consuming panic attacks. This morning, I was making breakfast and something about the color of the egg yolks set me off. The yolks were too yellow, nearly orange, like the contrast was turned up on a computer image. Terror shot down my spine. All of a sudden, I was watching myself from the third person, ripped from my body, and the disassociation made me panic even more. I staggered a step back, away from the stove, and reached for my eyes—for the simulation goggles, to free myself. But there was nothing there. I was trapped. Madison had trapped me again, locked me back in Ametrine where she would torture me, humiliate me, forever. My mom found me on the kitchen floor, clawing at my eyes, crying while the eggs burned.

And now I'm supposed to sleep. How am I supposed to sleep?

I wait until I'm sure Petey's drifted off, until Mom and Lex bumble off to bed and their doors click shut. Then, smooth as a shadow, I slide out of bed and pick up my art box. Petey snores and snuffles. I tuck the box under one arm and creep into the living room.

A dull blue darkness coats the room, skimming over every surface. Lex won't turn on the heat until it gets down to freezing, so the house is cold, an autumn chill leaching through the walls. My head throbs distantly.

The windows watch me, black and sleek as water, reflecting my face back to me. My eyes seem dull, haunted. I flick on a lamp and sit down on the floor, leaning my back against the couch.

When I open the art box, everything in me falls silent. I run my hands over the newspaper clippings, the shreds of fabric, old postcards and sticky notes. A gentle weight lowers in my hips, keeping me on the ground. Keeping me here, somewhere real.

My fingers scratch against the gloss of a magazine page. It's an ad for some breakfast place on Newbury Street. A bright orange sunny-side-up egg dominates the image. I cut it out in slow, careful snips. It's funny, how the egg in the picture is both real and not real. Somewhere, at some point, that egg had existed. It was sculpted in a warm animal's body and then passed between careful human hands. It was arranged in front of a camera, positioned with painstaking care, and photographed. Somewhere, somehow, this egg had been real.

But this image has little of that realness left. The picture was contorted on a computer screen, the yolk turned into that frightening neon yellow, the grease edited out. It was transformed into an avatar of itself. Like Madison did to us, in Ametrine. Like she did to her parents. Like she did to me.

The worst part is that I liked it. Seeing myself smoothed out, perfect and convincing. Several times since coming home, I've grimaced at the mirror, wanted to burn the acne off my forehead and douse my scalp in fresh hair dye. I've wanted to look like I did in Ametrine again.

But I've also started to depend on my flaws. They remind me that I'm here, that this is real. I run a finger over the ridge of acne on my cheek and know that I made it out. My tongue flicks over the gap between my teeth, and it proves that I'm free.

I savor the click of the scissors, the gentle rip of paper. For hours, I separate images from their original places. A pile grows next to my feet. An advertisement for a dress in the exact shade of Madison's jumpsuit. The word HERE, torn out from a news article. A picture of a parrot that reminds me of the man selling memories. *Summer vacation!* he'd yelled. *Warm cookies by the fire! Hugs from your mom! All your best memories, get them right here!*

I hesitate over the image of an ocean wave. It arches up, tense and coiled and about to break, forever frozen into that moment of suspension.

It reminds me of Vanessa.

She will have heard about what happened. Madison attacking me in the warehouse. Devin blood-soaked, beneath the balcony. Amelia.

She must have heard about the video too—the one Madison shared, where I shit-talked every person at the party. She knows I helped spread the rumor about her and Chet last year.

I wince, ripping the ocean wave out of its magazine. I study its sharp lines, the outrageous shade of sapphire. I add it to the pile.

I can't tell at first, what shape is emerging from the scraps. But as I work, my thoughts stay with Vanessa, and Everly, and Jake, and all the other people at the party who I've attacked behind their backs. Guilt burrows between my ribs. I can't undo what I said about them. When you hear someone talk about you like that, it sticks with you. It drives in and makes a home under your skin. I should know.

The collage crinkles under my hands. Glue sticks to my fingers, runs down my wrists. Finally, I pull back and take it in.

It's a spiral. A colorful, twisting spiral, like the teeth of the invitation keys. All the pictures relate, in some way, to Ametrine. As I gaze at it, an idea begins to form.

Madison doesn't come back to school. Neither does the rest of her crew. A strange quiet slithers through the hallways, and their lunch table sits empty as a skeleton.

I'm on my own again, while Devin recovers. But I don't

hide in the art room or talk shit to try to make friends. I unpack my lunch alone in the courtyard. Wind rustles the dying leaves of the potted trees.

"Mind if I sit?"

Vanessa leans one hand against the lunch table, tilting her head at me. For a moment I'm too shocked to speak. I thought I would have to track her down.

"Absolutely," I say. "I mean—absolutely I don't mind. Not absolutely I—"

"I know." She flops into the seat and unzips her lunchbox. All her food is organized into perfect tiny squares of Tupperware. She pops one open and offers me a strawberry.

"They're on indefinite suspension," she says. She takes a bite of a strawberry. "Madison's crew."

"All of them?"

"All of them." She chews on the stem. "A bunch of parents are filing a lawsuit. It's a PR disaster." She makes a fake sad expression. "Poor Madison."

My mouth twitches. "Any word from her?"

"Nothing. She's off social media. No one's seen her around town. She's completely disappeared."

Fear flares through me. If she hated me before, I can only imagine how she feels now.

"Good," I say, making myself take a swig of water. "Maybe she's learning something."

"Yeah," Vanessa says, eyes distant. "Maybe."

I glance down at my hands and do a quick reality check. *I'm here.* I study the lines on my palm. I swallow, and feel my throat move. *This is real.*

The courtyard buzzes around us, students laughing and lounging in the grass. Every few seconds, someone's eyes slide to me. I'm used to people watching me; Madison made sure of that. But there's something new in their gazes now. Not derision, or pity. Something more like respect. As if they see someone strong. Someone interesting. Someone who took on Madison Pembroke, and won.

The guilt returns, tastes metallic in my mouth. It isn't that simple. I still have to make things right.

I reach into my backpack. "I, um. Made you something."

Vanessa raises her eyebrows. "What do you mean?"

I rustle around in my bag, feeling her watch me. I pull out a small, framed collage and hand it to her. It's one of the ones I made last night.

Vanessa takes it warily. She holds it out from herself, as if she expects it to bite her. "What is this?"

My cheeks blaze. "It's . . . I make collages. I made this from images that made me think of you. Like a messy, combined Pinterest board. I didn't—I didn't want you to think, after seeing that video, that I don't respect you. Or that I see you in a bad light. So I made this. I made one for everyone at the party."

Vanessa traces the frame with her finger. The images are all water and sky: Rippling rivers, glowing clouds, crashing waterfalls. Countless shades of a wild and perfect blue. A few words cut out from a used book, spelling out: RISE / HERE / IN THE SUN / UNAFRAID.

"It's in the shape of a spiral key," she murmurs.

"Yeah," I say.

She doesn't say anything else. A strange, conflicted expression works across her face.

I gnaw on my lip, anxiety burning down my back. Maybe using the spiral key shape was wrong. I don't want it to bring back bad memories. But I chose that shape, over and over for each collage, on purpose. I wanted to take what happened and transform it. I wanted to create something new from the ruins.

"Thank you," she says finally. "This is really—thank you."

"I'm not asking you to forgive me," I say. "I just didn't want any stupid shit I said to live in your head. You're a cool person."

A small smile tugs at her mouth. She nods, once, and then stands up to leave. "See you around?" she says.

I nod.

That evening, I borrow Lex's car to visit Devin—and take a wrong turn.

It's ridiculous. I haven't lived in Countrywood Court for years now. But when I see the gate's been left open, it happens out of instinct. I turn left instead of right, tap the gas instead of the brakes, and the old Honda puffs up the familiar road like we never left.

Some of the houses changed colors. I don't recognize the children playing in the wide, yawning yards. It's weird how the world keeps going on without you.

I slow down as the road bends, and my old house comes into view. Bright blue paint shines off the walls, freshly coated. A kid's trampoline waits in the front yard, surrounded by dandelions and clover.

A deep, slow ache expands in my belly. Madison and I spent so many hours in that house together. Despite everything, a part of me misses her. The brave, competitive little girl who played pretend with me in the front yard. The anxious goofball who told me all her secrets. The person I trusted most in the world.

I'll never get that version of Madison back.

As I drive closer, I imagine the ghosts of our childhood selves, chasing each other through the yard. Hair streaming out behind us. Laughing our heads off. Awash in the simplest certainty.

I could stop the car. I could pull into the driveway and idle for a moment, remembering this house, our friendship. I could sit, endlessly, in this feeling.

But I don't.

Instead, I turn on my blinker. I raise my eyes to the road and keep driving.

ACKNOWLEDGMENTS

THIS BOOK EXISTS BECAUSE OF THE INCREDIBLE TEACHERS, mentors, and comrades in my life: hands that intertwined, becoming a bridge. Every word was drawn from the well you dug with me. There's not enough paper in the world to properly thank every person who made this dream possible, but I want to begin here, with this, with you.

Laura Southern: you saw me, you believed in me, and you made this happen. I won't ever forget it, won't ever stop being grateful.

My fearless team at Viking, with Jenny Bak and AZ Hackett at the helm: you've infused this story with so much heat and intelligence. You've made this book *real*. Thank you, Jessica Jenkins, Abigail Powers, Gaby Corzo, Lily Qian, Miranda Shulman, and Maddy Newquist.

All the folks at Working Partners: Anna Carey, Blair Thornburgh, Lynn Weingarten, Marianna Baer, and Chelsea Eberly. Thank you for welcoming me into this world.

The many teachers over the years who nurtured my creativity and taught me how to tell a story, with special thanks to:

Misty Hyler, Barbara Meyers, Heather Tedder, Stephen Shane, Rajiv Mohabir, and Mary J. Molloy.

Megan Busbice and Brianna Cunliffe: you taught me so much about writing and friendship. We've grown in different directions, but the roots will stay, come hell or high waters.

My kind and hilarious parents, who always believed in me. Mimi, who taught me how to edit. Grandma Berk and Poppy, who always arrived with a new book to read. Thank you. I love you.

Levi and Ella: you're my earliest readers and oldest friends. Thank you for everything.

Thais: you are light.

Oscar: thank you for being my co-dreamer. You are the love of my silly little life.

I am deeply grateful for the land that held me through childhood, Cherokee territory in the ancient Appalachian Mountains, a place that taught me everything I know about love and language.

And, of course, thank you to the reader, for spending time with this story.